He was down there, all right.

At first, as I moved into the hall, it was almost like being blind. Moisture from the night and my nerves stuck my shirt to my back. In my hand I carried a piece of plumbing pipe I'd found in a storage closet. I'd made Donna stay behind.

I knew he might be any sort of vandal or vagrant, but I didn't think he was. I was beginning to form an impression of who he might be.

He came at me in an awkward tackle, getting me around the waist and putting me hard up against the wall. The pipe dropped from my hand, clattering in the darkness on the floor. Just before he kicked me in the side of the face, I heard Donna start screaming. . . .

Also by Edward Gorman
Published by Ballantine Books:

MURDER STRAIGHT UP

NEW IMPROVED MURDER

ROUGH CUT

MURDER IN THE WINGS

Edward Gorman

BALLANTINE BOOKS • NEW YORK

Library of Congress Catalog Card Number: 86-13795

ISBN 0-345-34313-1

This edition published by arrangement with St. Martin's Press, Inc.

Manufactured in the United States of America

First Ballantine Books Edition: December 1987

735429

For my partner in crime,
Bob Randisi

"... there are men whom one hates until a certain moment when one sees, through a chink in their armor, the writhing of something nailed down and in torment."

—Gerald Kersh

1

By THE TIME WE REACHED THE SECOND ACT THE audience was well aware of what was going on.

Stephen Wade, the television star who was playing the role of the father in this version of O'Neill's *Long Day's Journey Into Night*, was so drunk that he was knocking against furniture and quite often forgetting his lines. Between acts he had been given coffee and a quick walk in the cold, damp May night, but neither had seemed to help much.

I wasn't quite sure how to feel. Because this was the first really serious play I'd ever been in, and because my performance as the drunken elder brother, James Tyrone, Sr., depended so much on what Wade did, I was angry most of the time I was on stage. But then I'd look closely at Wade, at the matinee-idol good looks that had slipped into white hair and booze-loosened flesh, and I'd feel sorry for him. There was a grief in his blue eyes that overwhelmed me sometimes and I sensed a man destroyed and left empty.

Among the people at the Bridges Theater, staff and cast

alike, there had been a lot of apprehension about how Wade, who had begun his career thirty years earlier in this same theater, would behave when he got here.

Well, for four weeks, he had done fine. From what anybody could tell, he stayed dry, his performances as impressive as anything we'd ever seen him do. On a couple of occasions he had asked Donna and me out to dinner, and we became friends of sorts. He always made her sad, his melancholy aura pulling her in, but he made her laugh, too. He was a great storyteller, and he'd known everybody important in Hollywood for the past twenty-five years. When the play finished its month-long run, I was going to take him fishing, up to a cabin a police officer friend of mine owned.

Then, he got drunk and came on stage that night and things changed.

A lot if it, I don't remember. I was aware of three things simultaneously—how awkwardly Wade was moving around the stage, how nervous I was that I was going to muff my own lines, and the steady undercurrent of whispers and snickers from the audience whenever Wade made a mistake.

Finally, it ended. The curtain came down and we all left the stage.

Michael Reeves, the director, was waiting in the wings. "Wade, I want to see you a minute." From the tremor in his voice, I could hear that Reeves was barely controlling his anger. He was six feet tall and muscular like a dancer. He might have been handsome if his swarthy face hadn't been so petulant. No matter what we did, he always seemed vaguely displeased. He never laughed except at somebody else's embarrassment.

When Reeves spoke, the whole cast stopped its quick flight to the dressing rooms. Much as Wade had embarrassed us, I sensed a protectiveness among the cast. Reeves was going to be very ugly.

Reeves came over and stood in front of Wade. "You realize you're fired."

Wade, still lost in a boozy haze, looked up and said, "I'm sorry about tonight. There's no excuse."

Reeves looked at the rest of us. "You see how he's going to try to get out of this? He's going to play the pathetic."

Wade, who was five-nine at best, tried to draw himself up with dignity, but he didn't have much luck. His shoulders slumped and his gut drooped. He was fifty-three years old and tapped out. He put out his hand for Michael to shake and said, "I embarrassed you tonight and I'm sorry." His voice quavered. I'd worked with enough alcoholics during my years on the force to know that Wade was very near the end. He probably needed hospitalization.

Reeves didn't take Wade's hand. Instead he slapped him.

Even above the noise the stagehands were making closing the theater down for the night, the slap sounded loud and harsh in the small theater.

"You sonofabitch!" Reeves screamed, letting his rage go. "This is an important play for me and you ruined it. Totally fucking ruined it!"

"Hey, Michael, down out a little, all right?" said Richard Keech, the actor who played Edmund. Keech had a suffering, almost pretty face wrapped in curly auburn hair.

"Yes, please, Michael. Let him go to his dressing room." This was Anne Stewart. Regal, slender, still a beauty at fifty, she played the mother with a quiet ferocity that had impressed us all.

"I don't think it's fair to pick on Michael. He isn't the one who's drunk." Evelyn Ashton, who played the maid, was twenty-four and ridiculously beautiful. Really. Since I'd met her I'd been playing a little game—trying to find a bad angle to her face. But there wasn't one. She had the gold silken hair of a storybook princess and gray eyes that were as luminous in their way as precious stones. Aerobics kept her body equally lovely. She had only one failing: she was obviously and painfully in love with Michael Reeves.

Now she started to slide her arm protectively around his waist, but Reeves pushed her away. He was trying hard to get control of himself. "I want you to take your things and get the fuck out of here tonight. Do you understand me?" He was yelling in Wade's face.

All Wade could do was stand there and take it. I glimpsed his eyes and wished I hadn't.

I was about to step in—I didn't like Reeves and maybe I was half using this as an excuse to finally have it out with him—when David and Sylvia Ashton appeared.

The Bridges Theater had been so named for one of the wealthiest men in the city, a man who'd made millions in steel when steel was building the country. His name was Hughton Bridges. Sylvia Ashton's mother, Leonora, had had the good sense to marry the man. Sylvia, and consequently her husband David, were very wealthy. They spent their days running the theater.

David Ashton was a mild man given to bankerish three-piece suits and a perpetual sad smile. One could see, though, the fading good looks that had once helped him in his own stage career. When he saw what was going on, he said to Reeves, "I wish you wouldn't make things any worse than they already are."

"I've fired him, David, and I expect you to back me up on it."

Ashton looked pained. He hated confrontations and Reeves was pushing him into a bad one. "Why don't you and Stephen and I go to my office and discuss this?"

Reeves, probably rightly, sensed that Ashton was going

to try to ameliorate the situation. "Goddamn you, David, why don't you show some balls for once? This has-been embarrassed all of us tonight and he should be fired for it!"

The small sob had the force of a gunshot.

Everybody turned to look at Sylvia Ashton. She was a frail woman of about her husband's age, maybe forty-five, with one of those too-delicate faces that suggests a mask. Her dark eyes had a quality of quiet madness. She seemed to see beneath surfaces, and what she saw there had unhinged her somehow. People around the theater spoke carefully of her stays over the years in various mental hospitals. Obviously, this was exactly the kind of pressure that got to her. In a sad but rather grand way, she said, "I thought we were all like a family here. We should be, you know. We all love acting more than anything else."

Reeves sighed, exasperated.

Anne Stewart, who was a good friend of Sylvia's, touched the smaller woman gently on the shoulder. Tears were shining in Anne's eyes.

But curiously, it was Wade who looked the most overwhelmed by Sylvia's obvious struggle with this moment. His head was down and he was shaking it side to side, like a penitent in a confessional. When he raised his head, his gaze was fully as forlorn as Sylvia's own.

Reeves pushed him then.

None of us expected it, and I doubt that Reeves meant the push to be that hard. Wade fell back into a grand piano. You could hear its impact with his back. A cracking sound, bone against wood. Then he fell to the floor, his arms flailing out comically.

What surprised me was how quickly he got up. What didn't surprise me was how angry he was.

Wade's reaction to Reeves's taunting had been atypical, perhaps because Wade had been ashamed of his drinking.

Maybe he felt that he had no choice but to suffer Reeves's anger. But, according to twenty years of press reports, Wade had a furious temper. He'd been taken to court many times for brawling.

Now I could see that temper.

Before I could get to him, he'd arced an impressive right hand into Reeves's face, startling and hurting the taller man, and slamming him into the wall.

Wade stalked in closer, set to throw more punches at Reeves. Wade, his face red, his eyes crazed for the moment, spittle at either side of his mouth, was frightening to watch. Enraged drunks usually are, as any cop will tell you.

I grabbed Wade before he could get his next punch off. He was all curses and craziness. Keech came over and helped me keep him away from Reeves. For his part, Reeves pushed his face into David Ashton's face and said, "You choose, David—him or me." He jabbed a sharp finger into Ashton's chest and then stormed off.

By now Sylvia was weeping openly, and Anne Stewart was holding her carefully, as if she might break.

I said to Wade, "Why don't you let me give you a ride to your hotel?"

But he was still very drunk and very angry. "I don't want shit from you, Dwyer. Not shit."

Everybody looked at me. There wasn't much to say.

I was the first one back to the dressing rooms. I got myself ready for the street and left.

2 To date Donna Harris has published only six issues of *Ad World*, which means that she has yet to master everything required to put out a magazine that caters to the Illinois advertising industry. When she's gathering material and writing, she's great company, as usual. But the closer publication day comes, the more her office becomes a minefield of layouts, photos, odds and ends of manuscript, Hardee's wrappers and empty Tab cans, and she gets to a point where she might pick a fight with Mother Teresa. The pressure gets to her and she doesn't mind sharing it.

After the scene at the theater, I drove around the city, letting the FM jazz station soothe me with some Mulligan doing the theme from *Exodus* (if you don't think artists can change pop lead into jazz gold, listen to that one) and tried to recognize what was happening to the downtown area.

Three bridges lead into the Loop area proper. Now, in May, Chicago was again transforming itself from the steel of winter to the breezes of spring, the promise of new foliage as vast as the lake that spanned the horizon.

In the cold rain the Loop was finishing up for the night, with only a few trendy spots still shaking a fist at midnight. I waved to a few squad car cops who knew me from my own cop days. They looked bored. Loop duty isn't a lot of fun.

By the time I drove past Donna's office, which is outside the Loop, I was no longer pissed at Wade, if I ever had been exactly. I liked the bastard, couldn't help it, and so did Donna. Now I was worried about what he'd do next. *Variety* would certainly carry the story about how he'd been fired from a small theater in the boonies. It was just the kind of ammunition West Coast casting directors would need to shut him off for good.

I drove into the parking lot at Donna's. Her car was gone. I felt one of those inexplicable pangs of betrayal. I really needed her. Couldn't she sense that through telepathy or some damn thing?

"You're really in a bad mood, aren't you?" I said after she opened the door in her robe and curlers and stood, hip cocked, glaring at me.

"I will be if you start that number again," she said in her best severe voice.

The "number" she referred to was how I'd simply pointed out that she became intolerable the closer she got to deadline. I'd once made the same observation about the first few days of her period, but she got so mad—I mean fucking crazed—that I knew better than to ever bring that up again.

There was a long and nervous silence. I saw her ironing board up behind her—she hates ironing the way I hate making beds—and the TV was on. It was Elizabeth Taylor in *Butterfield 8*.

"You could always invite me in."

8

"Well, you can see the kind of shape the place is in."

"Yeah, and you know how much I care about that sort of thing."

"You sound kinda down."

"I am, I guess."

"Well," she said. "I mean, to be real honest, Dwyer, you think we should be together tonight?"

"Why not?"

"Well, even though I think your routine about me being crabby the closer I get to deadline is all in your imagination, the rain has sort of got me down. Or something. I mean I was sitting there watching a Fritos commercial and I just burst into tears. A Fritos commercial."

"It's the rain."

"Don't sound so goddamn smug."

"Jesus, Donna, lighten up."

"And don't tell me to lighten up."

"All I said," I said, "was that it's the rain. You know how you get."

"And you don't get that way?"

"Well, sort of I do."

" 'Sort of.' "

I shook my head. Right then I felt like an orphan. "Maybe you're right. Maybe tonight's not a good night to get together."

She hadn't lightened up any. "Yeah, maybe you *are* right."

"Well," I said, wanting her to stop me. But she didn't. "Well, good night, Donna." I knew better than to try to kiss her.

"Good night, Dwyer." And with that she closed the door.

I went down the stairs, feeling very sorry for myself. I was about twenty feet down the walk, the cold rain combining now with fog, when I heard a window being pushed up.

"God, Dwyer, I'm sorry. I really am."

I turned around. I had no shame. "So can I spend the night?"

But that only irritated her again. "Why don't you just tell everybody in the apartment house that we sleep together?"

I cupped my hands. "Donna Harris and a guy named Dwyer are sleeping together."

"You asshole."

"So can I come up?"

"You asshole."

I took that to mean I could come up.

It wasn't the sort of lovemaking you read about in Judith Krantz novels. I mean, in terms of the old amore, we've certainly had better nights. I wanted to and she didn't want to, then she wanted to and I didn't want to, then neither of us wanted to, and then both of us wanted to, so we did—but by that time it was doomed to be less than wonderful. Holding each other afterward was actually better than the sex, holding each other and listening to the rain on the roof and watching the shadows of trees play in the streetlight and toss silhouettes across her bedroom walls like magic lanterns.

"I'm sorry it wasn't better for you," she said after a long time. It was the first time all night she had sounded glad to see me.

"Hey, I'm sorry it wasn't better for you. At least I had an orgasm."

"Well, I had an orgasm, too."

"You did? Really?"

"Well, something like an orgasm anyway."

Which meant that she hadn't had an orgasm at all but was

being sweet and her being sweet there in the darkness really cranked me up again and when I got cranked up she got cranked up and this time it was really kick-ass good, the way it can be only when you're loving somebody you truly love.

"Boy," she said afterward. "Boy."

"I take it it was better that time."

"You just want a compliment," she said and then promptly fell asleep without giving me one.

I was on the bottom of an ocean, chained to a rock the size of a house. I was being called urgently to the surface but I couldn't escape, hard as I tried.

I woke up realizing that the phone was ringing. It was on my side of her bed. She had her arms flung wide and was snoring. She was the only woman I'd ever known who could snore cute. I got the phone.

There was a long pause on the other end, a heavy-breather pause. I wondered if it might be a twist-o, or her ex-husband, the very wonderful (just ask him) Chad. But it wasn't.

He was very drunk and he had to say it twice before I could understand what the hell he was saying.

" 's big trull. 's big big trull."

Big big trouble.

I remembered my police training. When you talk to somebody drunk or desperate, stay calm.

"Where are you?"

" 's one piece 'a trull I won't get outta."

"Stephen, where are you?"

Another long pause. I heard a match being struck. In the receiver it sounded like a bomb going off.

"Where are you?" I repeated.

11

The cigarette had apparently helped a bit. At least I could understand him on the first sentence now.

"I'm at his apartment."

"Whose apartment?"

"Reeves's."

"Reeves's? Stephen, what the hell are you doing there?"

By now Donna was awake, whispering, "Is he all right?" She had a daughterly affection for Wade. At moments such as these it would translate into terror.

"Came over to 'pologize," he said.

"So what happened?"

There was a long sigh and then a silence and then a sigh again. "Fucker's dead."

"Dead?"

Another sigh. When he spoke again, he sounded miserable and lost. He sounded on the verge of tears. "I don't know what happened over here, Dwyer. Please come over right away. Please."

With that, he hung up the phone.

3 THE CLOSER WE GOT TO REEVES'S APARTMENT, THE more Pizza Huts and Hardee's and Long John Silver's we saw. In the rain all the neon had a certain beauty.

Reeves lived in a neighborhood on the edge of what had once been the Czech section of the city. Now some of the Czechs had moved out (literally), looking down on the houses they'd left behind—houses today occupied by people with NRA and country-and-western radio station stickers on their bumpers. It had become a lower-class white bastion. Blacks knew better than to move in. Reeves's place was just on the dividing line. White upper-class couples had recently started refurbishing some of the rambling old houses into mock-Victorian apartment houses. We found Reeves's building.

The run through the rain, from the driveway to the porch, got us soaked. In the vestibule we looked for his name along the row of ten mailboxes, and then we went up the curving staircase. The place smelled of fresh paint.

Reeves's apartment was in the rear. A silver number *11* identified it. If you looked closely, you could see that the door was ajar.

"Boy," Donna whispered, taking my hand and placing it over her breast. "Feel my heart."

It was racing, pounding, and I didn't blame it a damn bit.

I eased the door open. It squeaked so loudly I could imagine lights going on all over this side of town.

"Maybe we should just call the police," she whispered again.

"Don't you want to help Wade?"

I knew that would get her. She looked instantly guilty. She liked and, more importantly, felt sorry for Wade. She made a grim little expression with her mouth and nodded for me to proceed.

The first thing I noticed inside was the aquarium. It surprised me only because Reeves spent so much time playing the cool theatrical wizard. What the fuck would a cool theatrical wizard be doing with a tank full of fishies?

Light from the big fish tank was the only illumination in the front room. The rest of the place ran more to my expectations. The walls were decorated with posters from plays he'd directed as well as photographs of himself and the semi-famous actors he'd worked with at the Bridges Theater. Bookcases made of bricks and boards ran the length of the rear wall and were crammed with plays and quality paperbacks by writers as varied as Aristophanes and Neil Simon. That was the only time Simon would ever keep company with Aristophanes.

The furniture reminded me of my own stuff. A green couch that didn't at all match the green overstuffed chair that clashed with the dark blue drapes. In other words, a salute to Goodwill stores everywhere.

Three halls led off from the living room. One went to the kitchen, which was empty and smelled of dishes left in the sink for days. Another went to a screened-in porch at the back that smelled of new spring grass and rain. The third hall led to his bedroom and that's where we found him, sprawled across the bed. A butcher knife stuck out from between his shoulder blades, and a dark puddle of blood had seeped from the wound.

As Donna and I moved closer she started saying "Boy" and then "God," and then alternating the expressions back and forth the closer we got.

The bedroom was sparsely decorated—a few more play posters, a few more photos of himself with the famous. A clothes hamper stood open. Apparently he washed his clothes about as often as he did his dishes. I angled away from the smell.

"That's how I found him," a rough voice said from behind us.

Stephen Wade, dressed in a dark turtleneck sweater, a hound's-tooth Stanley Blacker sport coat, and a pair of dark pleated slacks, stepped from the walk-in closet looking dapper and very theatrical, as if he was playing a role in a British crime drama. To complete the image, he waved a .45 at us.

"God, Stephen," Donna said, "what's the gun for?"

I turned on a table lamp. He was sobering up fast, but a kind of madness, founded on fear I suppose, was setting in. His gaze was narrow and furtive. I wanted to say something to help—to calm him, to get that goddamn look out of his eyes—but nothing came to mind.

Donna started over to him. Maybe it was because her father had never been home when she was a child and as a consequence she secretly felt she'd never really had a father. Maybe it was because, with his large, handsome, silver-haired head, Wade looked like the ultimate TV-commercial father—or grandfather. Or maybe I was full of beans and she just plain old had a crush on him. Whatever it was, being around Wade sort of unglued Donna, and she got real maternal. Now, as she moved toward him, she held out her hand for him to give her the gun.

He took her in his arms and they hugged. I heard her sob, and for a moment I saw him close his eyes in a kind of surrender to her presence, but then he gently pushed her away and said, "I don't think I killed him, but I'm not sure."

"Oh, Stephen," she said, "you couldn't have killed him. You just couldn't." She turned back to me. "Tell him, Dwyer. Tell him he couldn't have killed him."

"I appreciate you confidence," Wade said. "I just wish I could share it."

I looked at the body and then at Wade. His eyes seemed worse by the minute. The soberer he got, the more shock set in.

"Why don't we go out into the living room?" I said.

"I'll make some coffee," Donna said. Then she remembered. "Boy, I wouldn't want to drink any coffee made in that kitchen. How about if I walk down to that Pizza Hut and get some coffee?"

"Great idea," I said.

While Donna left, I led Wade into the living room. For a long minute he said nothing. He just stared at the fish—gold and red and blue and green—slapping their whispy little tails through the water. At the moment they seemed to have it knocked. All they had to do all day was swim around and eat food that looked like crunched up communion wafers. They didn't have to worry about murders or being a drunk or has-been actor or a security cop who couldn't think of a damn thing to say to help out a friend.

"For what it's worth," I said finally, "I don't think you did it, either."

He smiled sadly. "I don't deserve friends like you two. I really don't."

We were silent again for a time. The aquarium bubbled. Cars went by in the rain outdoors. The wood of the house started to smell sweet and damp, the way old wood does in rainstorms. The fishies didn't say a damn word.

"You going to tell me about it?" I asked gently.

"Not much to tell." He ran a hand across his face. "Actually, I don't remember much at all. After the show tonight, I went back to my hotel room and really started feeling sorry for myself. I ordered a bottle up from room service and started in on it. Somewhere during that time I got the bright idea of trying to make amends with Reeves. I'm not kidding myself, Dwyer; if word gets back to Hollywood that I fell off the wagon during a show, I'm done. All done, my friend." He shrugged. "So anyway— you know how you get bright ideas while you're very drunk—I thought maybe if I came over and personally apologized to Wade, he'd come around. I was so drunk that I completely overlooked that he'd throw me out the minute he saw how drunk I was." He passed his hand over his face again. The .45 was still in his hand. "But I came over. I dimly remember taking a cab. I came up to the door here— I'd been here once before for a party—and the rest of it I'm not sure about. I'm afraid it's lost in the booze."

I tried to keep the anxiety out of my voice, but I couldn't. "Stephen, you've got to think hard about it. Very hard."

"It's a blank. A complete goddamn blank except for a couple of images."

"Images of what?"

"I think—I wish I could be sure of this—I think when I came in I just sort of opened the door and walked right in and that's when somebody pushed me down."

"Knocked you out?"

"No. That's not my impression, anyway. More like pushed me out of the way."

"And then what?"

"Then the next thing I'm sure about is waking up and not knowing where I was at first and then finding Reeves in the bedroom. With the knife in his back."

"Did you touch him?"

"Reeves? I think so."

"Try to think, Stephen. It's important."

"I think when I saw him I went a little crazy and tried to pull the knife out."

"Shit."

"Bad, huh?"

"Real bad. Your prints are on the knife."

"Could we wash them off with something?"

"From what you're saying, I'm not sure it would matter. You took a cab over here, which means there's a cabbie who will testify to bringing you here, and any number of Reeves's neighbors could have seen you here." I nodded to the .45. "So where did the weapon come from?"

"I always carry it."

"Always?"

"Yeah. Too many creeps in the world."

"Not smart, Stephen. Not smart at all. Particularly with your problems with the bottle."

There was a tiny knock on the door. I got up. Wade raised the .45.

Donna came in with a big white Pizza Hut paper bag. She was wet and shivering. After she handed us our coffees she went into the bathroom. I heard a blow drier.

Wade sat in the light of the aquarium and drank his coffee and held the .45 in firing position and looked worse and worse. I was sitting there staring at the floor when he started crying.

Maybe because he always plays the patriarch, maybe because in person he's so traditionally manly, I'd just never thought of Wade as crying. But he did and it was terrible to watch and hear because he didn't know shit about crying; he was worse at it than I was. He'd start to cry and then he'd stop and then he'd start again. He sounded more as if he were choking or starting to vomit than crying, but he kept on and finally I could see that his cheeks were wet. That was just when Donna came out and you can imagine how she reacted.

"Oh, God, Stephen, oh, God," she said and plopped herself down next to him and threw her arms around him. His coffee spilled all over the floor but she kept hugging him anyway. That seemed to help in the crying department, but by then he was sobbing and there was a kind of enviable freedom in the noise of it. It was sort of like getting all your past sins and shame out and starting life all over again.

"I've fucked it up, I've fucked it all up," he said over and over again, and she only held him tighter.

I sat there watching and sipped my coffee. Every once in a while Donna would look over at me and shake her head as if Wade was our baby and he had the measles bad or something. I couldn't help but agree with him; he had fucked it up—four marriages, enough children to fill an orphanage, fistfights and paternity suits and broken contracts, all the while doing very little to nourish the enormous talent God or his genes had given him gratis. As much as I liked him, I almost couldn't forgive him for the waste he'd made of his talent.

When he finished he was very calm—almost eerily so. He got up and went into the john. Then we heard him piss, and we heard the water run for a long time.

"God, Dwyer, I don't know what to do," Donna said. With the water running we didn't need to whisper.

"Neither do I."

"You don't really think he did it, do you?"

"I don't know."

"But if he had a gun, why would he have stabbed him?"

"That's a good question, Donna."

"You're going to call the cops, aren't you?"

She made it sound as if I'd said I was going to hand our baby over to the A-1 Child Molestation Agency.

"I have to," I said.

She sighed. "Sometimes I wish you hadn't ever been a cop. You know?"

"Yeah." She understood why I had to call the police.

"Well, at least call Edelman."

Donna and Edelman liked each other.

"Yeah, that's what I was thinking."

Wade came out. He had shaved and used some goop on his hair and straightened his clothes. He looked sober and ready for a night on the town. The .45 remained in his hand.

"I'm going," he announced.

I'd half expected him to say that. "Stephen, that'll just make things worse."

"I don't have any choice. They're going to wrap it up nice and tidy and not even consider the possibility that I'm innocent."

Donna got up and went to him. This time he wouldn't let her near. "I couldn't ask for better friends than you two. I really couldn't. But for now I'm going to have to operate on my own."

I got up, too. I had a vague idea about lunging at him and getting the gun.

He raised the .45. "I wouldn't kill you, Dwyer, because you're a pal, you really are. But I would shoot you in the leg or something." He looked at me. He was sad and scared and confused. "You better take my word for it, kid, 'cause I fucking mean it."

I didn't doubt him at all.

He opened the door. He looked at me and then at Donna. She broke into horrible tears. And then he was gone.

I got her over to the couch and helped her lie down and tried holding her to stop the tears—she was shaking in a way that terrified me. Then I went to the phone and woke up Edelman.

EDELMAN ARRIVED HALF AN HOUR LATER, TEN minutes behind two other men from Homicide Division, half a dozen uniformed officers, a trio from the medical examiner's, and two baffled-looking young people from the press. At this time of night they were usually sitting at word processors entering a bunch of stuff that stringers provided them. They'd never handled a felony before, let alone a murder involving a famous actor from Hollywood.

Edelman still had sleep marks tatooed on his left cheek, and his thinning brown hair had been plastered down with King Kong hair spray in an effort to make it lie flat. Beneath the bottom of his trench coat you could see baggy gray work pants. He kept the coat buttoned up to his neck, which meant that he was probably wearing his pajama top. Maybe the one with the boats on it, which his wife had gotten him for his last birthday as a joke. "But you know, Dwyer," she'd told me that night at the party (a party for the Edelmans is a birthday cake and Kool-Aid for their tribe of five kids), "he just looked at them and said 'These are great, honey.' He didn't think the little boats were funny at all."

Now Edelman said, "Hastings said you've already given your statement."

I nodded.

"Doesn't sound like it's going to be too hard to put together," Edelman said.

"Hi," Donna said. She'd gone down to Pizza Hut again after the rain stopped. More coffee. She handed one to me and one to Edelman.

"You should've been a nurse."

"Can't stand the sight of blood," she said. Then, realizing the circumstances, "I guess that isn't very funny." She watched Edelman sip his coffee. He looked like a grade school principal. He was a gentle man, and wise in his way, and maybe the best male friend I'd ever had. When he finished sipping, Donna said, "Did Dwyer tell you?"

He was still sleepy. He seemed confused, as if he'd missed something. "Tell me what?"

"About Wade."

"What about him?"

"How he didn't do it."

"Didn't kill Reeves, you mean?"

She nodded.

He raised his eyes to me. He looked sad. For Donna. "Well, let's wait till we get all the reports in, all right?"

"Do you think he did it?" Donna asked.

He glanced at me again. "I don't want to hurt your feelings, Donna."

"So you do think he did it, huh?"

"I'd have to say it's a pretty good bet. He certainly had a motive. And he came over here."

"But somebody pushed him down."

22

She sounded young and naive. I wanted to hug her, protect her. Edelman did it for me. He put his arm around her shoulder and gave her a little tug and said, "We'll wait for the reports, okay?"

Half an hour later the whole neighborhood was alive with press. Three TV stations showed up with vans. In the cold, and by now clear May morning—cold enough to kill the early flowers—their lights were ominous.

I'd watched all the processes. Things looked worse and worse for Wade. They'd found the cabdriver who'd brought him over. The cabbie gave a positive ID. A neighbor upstairs said she'd heard Wade go into Reeves's apartment and then heard a scuffle shortly afterward. The knife was removed from Reeves's back and put into a plastic bag. The knife would have Wade's fingerprints all over it.

I went out on the back porch. The smell of new-mown grass was on the air. The dawn was pink and yellow behind the thunderheads. Donna sat across from me on an empty Pepsi case. I'd asked Edelman to come out when he was finished talking with the detective in charge.

He came out with a cigar in his mouth. Unlit. "One of the guys had a baby. Or rather, his wife did. I hate the smell of these when they're lit, but the tobacco tastes pretty good just to chew on." He was obviously trying to avoid what he had to say to us. "He looks pretty good for it, Dwyer."

"How good?"

"Real good."

"What's going to happen?"

"APB. Armed and dangerous. He drinks and you tell me he's got a weapon."

"Yeah."

"We don't have a hell of a lot of choice."

Donna stood up. She was shaking again.

"Why don't you take her home, Dwyer?"

I nodded.

Donna said, "You wouldn't shoot him, would you?"

Edelman went over and put his arm around her again. "I just wish he hadn't run, Donna. That really complicates things."

"Yes," she said, her voice almost gone. "Yes, I know."

5 SEVEN HOURS LATER I WAS STANDING AT A DISPLAY OF sunglasses, watching in a mirror a man thinking about taking a watch from the jewelry counter. After breakfast Donna had gone to *Ad World* to wrap up the current issue and I'd come here, to Sparkle City (yes, indeed), where I was presently a wage slave for the American Security company.

Lunch I got from a machine. At three, when I'd finished my four-hour shift, I headed straight for home and my jogging clothes. The only way I would get through the rest of the day without sleep was to run a few miles.

By seven o'clock, showered and dressed in a buttoned-down white shirt without a tie, a tweed sport coat with one button missing, and a pair of jeans that hadn't exactly come wrinkle-free from the drier, I pulled my rusting Honda Civic up in front of the Bridges Theater.

The marquee was dark. Inside the locked front doors, the light from the stage was glowing dimly into the lobby. Somebody was in there. I went around to the alley and tried the side door. Locked. I knocked. Stan DeVoto, the janitor, opened up.

"Hey, Dwyer, what're you doin' here? Figured you woulda heard they closed down for the night."

"Yeah. Ashton left word with my service."

He smiled. He was in his sixties, bald and beer fat, and I would have given at least one of my testicles to be as happy as he usually seemed. Nuclear war? Piss on it; the Cubbies are on this afternoon (though come to think of it, the way the Cubbies play sometimes, nuclear war might be more enjoyable to contemplate). He always talked about the "mizzus" and where a guy could get Blatz on the cheap (but never cheap enough for my taste) and who among the actors was a "good guy." He never said who wasn't a good guy, but you could tell what he thought by the way his mouth tightened and he squinted his spaniel eyes.

"They're all inside," he said.

"You mean the cast?"

He nodded. "David, he told me nobody would be coming over, but they all seemed to drift in." He smiled. "Just like you."

I shook my head. "I suppose we're all in a state of shock."

"Yeah, like that guy Lockhart."

I didn't know who he meant. "Who's that?"

"One of Reeves's friends." The way he said "Reeves" told me that death hadn't changed his mind about Reeves. He'd never been one of the "good guys." (Reeves treated most people pretty badly unless there was something he wanted from them.) "Came in here like he was in a daze. Seemed all broke up. Kinda felt sorry for him."

"What'd he want?"

"Wanted to see Michael's office. Hell, the cops were here

earlier in the day, so I didn't figure there'd be any problem lettin' him in, you know."

"So you let him in?"

He could sense that maybe he hadn't done the right thing. "They were buddies, Dwyer."

"All right," I said.

But he wasn't finished defending himself. "Seems Lockhart was one of Reeves's convict friends. You know that acting class he teaches? Lockhart's one of those guys."

"All right, Stan."

He rubbed his bald head. "I fucked up, huh?"

I shrugged. "That's how I've spent my life, Stan, fucking up. It isn't anything to worry about."

"I won't let the s.o.b. in there next time—if he ever comes back, I mean. You can bet your ass on that."

"Great."

"I thought there was something fishy about him, Dwyer. I really did."

"See you, Stan."

In case you don't already know, Eugene O'Neill's *Long Day's Journey Into Night* is the autobiographical drama of America's greatest playwright. It's his tortured recollection of his mother, a morphine addict, his father, an insensitive cheapskate, and his brother, a doomed alcoholic. In the inscription he wrote to his wife Carlotta, O'Neill says, "I give you the original script of this play of old sorrow, written in tears and blood." He ends by saying that at last he can "face my dead and write this play—write it with deep pity and understanding and forgiveness for *all* the four haunted Tyrones."

The tone of his inscription was the mood on stage when I reached it.

Evelyn Ashton and her mother Sylvia and her father

David sat on the couch, while at the table Keech, who played my younger brother, sat with a beer in his hand. Anne Stewart, who played our mother, sat across from him. There was no conversation. They were just staring blankly. From the wings, I watched for a time. At one point Evelyn, even in blue jeans and a wrinkled white blouse the beautiful ingenue, put her head on her mother's shoulder and began crying softly. The rest of us had lost a director—she'd lost a lover. For some reason Keech looked irritated with her tears. He scowled in her direction, but then he met Anne Stewart's disapproving gaze and softened his expression.

When I came on stage, only David Ashton seemed much interested in me. He came over and poured me some wine from a bottle on the dining room table. While I waited for him to finish, I turned and looked out at the theater. There was something lonely about all those empty seats.

"Here you are, Dwyer. Glad you decided to show up." He leaned in so his daughter wouldn't hear him. "I suppose we're holding our own impromptu little wake here." He wore his standard blazer and white shirt. He had good features and his blond hair lent him an almost dashing quality. But there was something weak about him. I was never sure how to explain it. He struck me as a boy wearing his father's clothes. "Why don't you come over and sit down?"

I did, but the next ten minutes made me wish I'd done what Donna had wanted me to do, which was meet her at an Italian place for dinner and then go over to her place and watch a very good lost movie called *Who'll Stop the Rain*.

I don't know what was said; I hardly listened. I just responded on autopilot. Wasn't it terrible? Indeed it was. Could any of us have guessed that Wade was in such desperate straits? Indeed we couldn't have. Poor Michael; poor Evelyn; poor Bridges Theater. Indeed indeed indeed.

Keech said, "Have they found the cocksucker yet?"

Ashton said, "That sort of language is hardly called for. There are ladies here."

Keech, his curly hair like an aureole around his head, said, "Have they, Dwyer?"

"Not that I know of."

"And not that you'd give a shit, either."

"What's that supposed to mean?" I was tired and edgy enough that my temper responded before my brain did.

"Just that you're probably a lot more worried about Wade than about Michael. You and your girlfriend got pretty chummy with the drunken bastard."

Ashton said, "Do we have to argue among ourselves? Don't we have enough to feel badly about?" He had the whining intonation of a fourth-rate minister.

"Why don't you both shut up?" Evelyn snapped at us. "Anyway, Keech, you're a fine one to defend Michael."

"What's *that* supposed to mean?" Keech said.

"I was in the parking lot the other night when you tried to punch Michael. I suppose you call that being a good friend?"

It was as if Keech had been ready for her. He did it quick and he did it ugly. "I suppose now's not a good time to tell you about the girl Michael was keeping on the side."

"You're a liar!"

Keech laughed. "You know better than that, Evelyn. It's time you quit kidding yourself." Keech stood up, drained his bottle, and set it down. He was one of those little men who seem physically perfect—the sort who inevitably get called "cute"—but his size had made him insufferable. He was far too fond of himself. He looked around with what seemed to be pity and amusement and then said to me, "I hope they shoot the fucker, Dwyer. That's what he's got coming."

There wasn't anything to say to that kind of malice. There never is. To Ashton, he said, "Let me know when we'll do another performance." With that, he left the stage.

When he was sure Keech was gone, Ashton stood up and said, "Well, that wasn't very pleasant, was it?"

Evelyn looked at her father and shook her head. "Can't you just call him a name, Daddy? Do you always have to be so goddamn polite?"

Slyvia took her daughter's hand. "Dad hardly has that coming, darling." Sylvia's dark good looks were spoiled only by her mad eyes. Though nobody in the cast had been ungallant enough to say it, she was reminiscent of the mother in the play: living in her own world, dealing with the worst sort of atrocities but pretending there was absolutely nothing wrong. "Now apologize to your father."

Evelyn glared at the man. "I'm sorry, Daddy."

"I don't want to stoop to his level, that's all, honey."

Evelyn was not persuaded.

Anne Stewart stood up next. She was wearing a leotard and very tight Levi's. She had auburn, gray-streaked hair pulled back and tied up in a piece of Navajo jewelry the size of a fist. She had a nose that a queen would envy and dark eyes that you could study for a century and never quite figure out. She was fifty and sexy in a breathtaking way that not even Evelyn's beauty could match. "I guess I'll go, too," she said.

"No more wine?" David Ashton said.

Anne shook her head. "It's really getting to be a downer, I'm afraid."

"The rain isn't helping," Sylvia Ashton said.

Anne nodded in agreement. "Well, everybody, good night."

We all said our good nights.

When Anne was gone, Sylvia said, "Where do you suppose he went?" She stared at me.

"Wade, you mean?"

"Yes."

"I don't know."

"It said on the news tonight that you were the last person to see him."

"Me and my lady friend, yes."

She looked as sad as a child who'd just been told that her Daddy had died. "Do you suppose they'll kill him? Then Michael will be dead and Stephen will be dead."

You could hear it in her voice, whatever happened when she started on her inevitable path to the madhouse again. I felt sorry for her. I wanted to touch her in some way, just a reassuring touch, but that's always a bit difficult to do with a husband less than ten feet away.

Obviously David Ashton heard it in her voice, too. He jumped up as he'd jumped up many times in his life, and his hand went out, a life preserver of sorts. She took it without fuss or hesitation.

Even Evelyn stopped feeling sorry for herself long enough to say, "Come on, Mom, let Daddy and me take you upstairs and we'll watch some TV."

"Isn't Jack Benny on cable?" Sylvia wanted to know.

"Yes," Ashton said gravely. "Yes, darling, he is."

"Then let's hurry," Sylvia said. She sounded bright and happy all of a sudden. She also sounded spooky as shit.

"Thanks for coming by," Ashton said. He had one of those strong grips that bland men sometimes surprise you with. It was like sticking your hand in a vise. "I don't suppose we'll open again for a few days."

I pulled my hand away. It stung.

They left the stage. I stood and looked out at the empty theater again. Two years ago I'd been a cop, and that's all I wanted to be. Then I had gotten a part in a traffic safety spot and people started telling me how well I'd done. All of a sudden, being a cop wasn't enough. I wanted to be an actor.

Of course I'd had a wife back then, too. She hadn't understood and she'd found a man who hadn't understood right along with her, a good enough man that my fifteen-year-old son liked him a hell of a lot more now that the guy was his stepfather. I usually saw my wife when I picked our boy up. Recently, she had started looking as if she'd just discovered oil in her back yard. I don't think she ever looked that happy all the time we were married. Probably with good reason.

Behind the flats I heard the elevator taking the Ashtons to the top floor of the theater. There was a sprawling penthouse up there where they lived along with the matriarch of the clan, Mrs. Bridges. A nervous disorder had confined her to bed. I had never met her. Everybody assured me that I was lucky. I was told that her servants called her "Benito," after Mussolini.

My footsteps rang hollow as I left the stage and headed for the wings.

I was going to look up Stan and say good night and see if Donna was still awake enough to let me come over. It's fun to be in your forties and still live essentially the way you did in high school.

I was walking past the dressing rooms when I heard something at the top of the winding metal stairs that led to more dressing rooms and Michael Reeves's office. As the resident director here, he had been given space to conduct all his business affairs, including the commercials he directed for various ad agencies.

I raised my head. The lights upstairs were out.

Somebody tiptoed through the gloom above my head. A door yawned open. The tiptoeing stopped.

I thought of locating Stan and borrowing a flashlight. But maybe the visitor would be gone and I wouldn't find out who it was and what the person wanted. If I wanted to believe that Stephen Wade was innocent—and I did—then it was up to me to prove it.

I went up the stairs on tiptoes myself, cursing myself at each step for being such a water buffalo. The damp night caused me to sweat and the darkness made me stumble. I reached the stairway with almost no pride left. Light from the window at the east end of the hall showed me a corridor with four doors. I stood absolutely still. My heart sounded as if it needed a tuneup. My feet felt damp. I needed a shower; I needed help.

When the door opened, I leaned back into the shadows.

She stuck her lovely head out and looked first one way and then the other, and then she slowly came out. She must have thought I was gone. After checking the corridor for signs of life, she walked past me to the stairs and descended with utter grace and without making a sound. The police force could have used her.

After a few minutes I heard her saying good night to Stan, and then I heard the big metal side door squeak open. I ran to the window and watched as Anne Stewart got into her Mercedes and drove off.

What the hell had she been doing in Michael Reeves's office, I wondered as I went downstairs.

I was nearing the stage door when I heard the phone ring and Stan answer it. He said, "I don't know, Mr. Ashton. I think he may already have gone. Yes, sir. Yes, sir. Good night, sir."

He hung up just as I reached him. "Oh, Dwyer. You are here, huh?"

"Unless I'm a ghost."

"That was Mr. Ashton."

"Oh?"

"Yeah, he said he thought you might still be down here. He said he wants you to come up to the penthouse."

"You're kidding?"

He shrugged. "That's what he said."

"Did he say what he wanted?"

"Nope."

"You think there's an emergency or something?"

"Not that I know of."

"I wonder what the hell's going on."

"There's a good way to find out." He smiled, nodding toward the elevator. "Get on the damn thing and go up there."

I smiled at him. "Good point."

I got on the elevator and went up. I was still wondering about Anne Stewart and what she'd been doing in Reeves's office.

6 EVEN BEFORE THE ELEVATOR DOORS HAD OPENED completely I saw a chandelier that cast an almost blinding light over a reception area nearly as large as the theater's. A fleshy man with sleek white hair and wearing a blue jumpsuit nodded hello. When he spoke it was in good English with a Latin American accent. "You are Mr. Dwyer."

"Yes."

"Mrs. Bridges would like to see you."

I looked around. Three hallways angled off from the reception area. Somewhere down the corridors lived the three Ashtons. The place seemed to be divided into three apartments.

"I'm not going to see David or Sylvia?" I asked.

"Mrs. Bridges did not mention them." He pointed to the second hallway. "She'll be most happy."

I followed him down a corridor so broad that it was almost a room itself. Discreetly lit lithographs by Klee and Picasso lined the north wall. On the other wall were photographs of the Bridges family, usually posed outside a factory or a store or a building that the family owned. For a family from a small Midwestern town they were exceptionally wealthy. Two presidents had selected family members to be foreign ambassadors; one president had even taken a Bridges into his cabinet.

The closer we got to the end of the hall, the sweeter the air became. Cloyingly sweet. When the servant in the blue jumpsuit stopped, I paused and sniffed the air.

"Flowers," he explained with a smile. "Many, many flowers."

The smell reminded me of a funeral parlor. When I got inside the room, I understood why.

Before my eyes settled on the banked rows of flowers, I saw the frail, almost cute little woman propped up in a huge bed covered with a pink brocaded bedspread. Amid all the flowers, the tiny woman reminded me of an illustration from *Alice in Wonderland*.

When I reached her, she stuck out a slip of a hand and put it in mine. It was like shaking with a kitten. She glanced at the man in the blue jumpsuit, and for the first time I saw the power of the Bridges family: he left the room instantly.

Before I devoted more attention to her, I finished inspecting the room. The flowers, roses and gardenias and mums, literally filled the room. With the thick gold drapes drawn and the door closed behind the servant, I felt as if we were out of time, existing on some altered plane between death and life—particularly when I saw the collage of old photographs next to her bed.

Calvin Coolidge doffed a derby; Ike smiled baldly; Nixon grinned nervously. Each was pictured with an arm around Hughton Bridges, who would have been this woman's husband. But that was not all. There was Ronald Reagan, Celeste Holm, Caesar Romero; there was Frank Sinatra and

Satchmo and Dinah Shore—each with both of the Bridges, Hughton and the woman before me, Leonora.

"I'm afraid I don't know many of the celebrities today," she said, drawing back my attention.

I smiled. "I'm afraid I don't, either."

"I noticed your nose."

"Pardon me?"

"Your nose." She giggled. "It wiggled. Like a rabbit's. It's the flowers. Not everybody likes them. I love them. But you don't." Her little blue eyes were flirtatious. In her pink silk nightgown it was still possible to see what a beauty she'd once been, the beauty she was still in the fading photographs. She said, "You're wondering how old I am."

I felt myself flush.

"Perfectly natural and perfectly understandable," she said. "I'm eighty-three."

"You look wonderful."

"Would I sound vain if I said I know I did?"

"Not at all."

"For somebody eighty-three I look damn wonderful, if you'll pardon my French."

So this was "Benito." I had no doubt, just looking at her, that the stories about her were true. But they left out one of the good parts. "Benito" was a charmer.

"You know what I did this afternoon? Something very foolish."

"What's that?"

"Do you remember a hillbilly comedienne named Judy Canova?"

"Vaguely."

"She made a lot of very cheap movies back in the forties and early fifties. Anyway, Hughton used to own some coal mines down South, and she was very popular there. So this afternoon I saw in the cable guide that one of her movies was being shown, and I watched it. I'd hoped it would bring back memories of my husband and I. We always had such great times down South. But you know what?"

"What?"

"It was a terrible, terrible movie. It was like watching a high school play."

I smiled. "I'm sorry."

"Oh, don't be sorry. It was a good lesson for me." She paused. "Most things are best just before or long after they've happened. Everything else is something of a disappointment, I'm afraid."

"I guess I'd have to agree with that."

She giggled again. "Good. You look like an intelligent man." She angled a knotty hand to a nearby stand. "There's Scotch in there if you'd like some. I keep it on hand for all my gentleman callers." She smiled. " 'Gentleman callers.' Tennessee Williams used that in *The Glass Menagerie*. I met him several times. Too bad he was a homosexual. He was quite charming. But then I've always liked the theater and theater people, and so did my late husband. That's why we've spent millions on the theater downstairs, bringing in actors who would never have dreamed of coming to the Midwest otherwise. Our theater is my obsession and was Hughton's most treasured possession." For half of her little speech, she looked up at the collage of photographs; for the second half she watched my face. I didn't know what she was looking for, and it made me self-conscious. "And now something terrible's happened to our theater, hasn't it, Mr. Dwyer?"

"I'm afraid it has."

"Scandal. The first in our thirty-five-year history." Her shiny eyes hardened the way they had with the servant. Then she said, "I phoned the police today. I wanted all the background I could get on the murder. I spoke with a

Detective Edelman. I hope you don't mind, but because the press reports said that you were the last one to see Stephen Wade, I asked Detective Edelman what he thought of you. Edelman is a Jewish name, isn't it?"

"In his case it is."

"I have nothing but respect for most of the Jewish people I know," she said. "And I'm sure I would feel just the same about Detective Edelman if we ever met in person. He was charming on the phone. Very patient with me. I'm an old lady and it couldn't have been much fun for him." She paused again, touching her tiny hand to her throat, as if trying to draw a deep breath. She looked like a dying kewpie doll. "He told me you don't think Stephen Wade is guilty," she said.

"That's right."

"You have proof of that?"

"Not yet."

"You really don't think he's guilty?"

"No, I don't."

"Then what are you going to do about it?"

"I'm not sure yet."

"I've drawn a check for you. One thousand dollars."

"For what?"

"To prove that Stephen Wade isn't guilty. To prove that nobody associated with the theater is guilty."

Finally I understood why she'd called me there, what she hoped to get out of our meeting. She wanted me to prove that the theater and its people were blameless in the murder of Michael Reeves.

"He was an unsavory sort, wasn't he?"

"I'm not sure who you mean, Mrs. Bridges."

"Michael Reeves, of course. He had far too many girlfriends, and he spent too much time working with those convicts." She fixed her eyes on me. "You'll accept my check?"

I shrugged. "I guess I'd just as soon you kept it. If I turn something up then you can give me something as a reward."

"Detective Edelman said you'd probably react that way. He said that all in all you were a very competent policeman."

"I was all right. Nothing special, really."

She smiled and held out her hand. I took it. Her eyes sparkled again. "I'm afraid at my age, I don't have my seductive powers anymore. In my youth I was very good at getting my way." She put her other hand on top of mine. "Won't you help me, Mr. Dwyer?"

"Your seductive powers aren't bad at all, Mrs. Bridges. Not at all."

A doorbell sounded discreetly. She touched a button next to her bed. The door opened. David Ashton came in. The change in her expression was so abrupt that it bordered on the comic. "Yes?" she said. "Can't you see I'm busy?"

"I'm sorry, Leonora." He was embarrassed in front of me. Nobody likes being talked to that way. Nobody should. She was a different woman now. I felt sorry for Ashton. He was a wimp, but there are worse things to be.

"So what is it you want?"

He cleared his throat. She'd humiliated him so much that he could hardly speak. "You said to keep you informed about Wade."

"Yes. What about him?"

"There was a bulletin on television just now. They think he was spotted in a supermarket about half an hour ago."

"Is that all?"

"Yes."

"Then good-bye, David."

"Yes, Mother."

He left as quickly as he could.

She said, "I don't suppose that was very nice."

"I'd agree with that."

"You sound angry."

"Nobody should be treated that way."

"I've been very good to David. Do you know his background?"

"Right now I don't particularly give a damn about his background."

"His father worked for Hughton as a chauffeur. David isn't the namby-pamby he pretends to be. I saw him angry one time that I especially remember. A director was very insulting to a set designer and David grabbed the man and threw him, literally threw him, against the wall. He's so good-looking that you overlook the fact that he keeps himself in great shape and is very strong.

"And for all his blandness, he's not without wiles. Don't forget that he spent many years as an actor and is capable of giving very good performances." She paused a moment, looking down some invisible tunnel at the past. "Just after my daughter Sylvia had one of her breakdowns, David pretended to befriend her. What he really meant to do was get her pregnant. Which is exactly what he did. Unfortunately, my husband and I were out of the country and didn't know what was going on. So she gave birth to Evelyn. David got rich." She consulted the old photographs again. "Hughton was so much against him that he wanted to fly Sylvia to Mexico for an abortion, but her psychiatrist—a family friend named Dr. Kern—was against it. He was afraid that losing the child would only drive Sylvia deeper into schizophrenia."

"He still doesn't deserve that kind of treatment."

"You're from his background, I suspect. Blue-collar?"

"My father worked in a factory."

She met my angry gaze. "It may surprise you, Mr. Dwyer, but my father was a groundsman."

"That does surprise me."

"I'm not a snob, Mr. Dwyer. But I don't like underhanded men. Which is what David is."

I checked my watch. "I need to be going, Mrs. Bridges."

She put out her hand again. This time I hesitated. Then I took it. "Don't decide yet."

"Don't decide what yet?" I asked.

"Whether you like me or not. You need more time."

Her game-playing had started to have some appeal again.

"All right. I'll give it a few days."

"I wish you'd take that check."

"We'll talk about it if I accomplish something. Okay?"

She looked at me and laughed. "Now you're the kind of man I wish *had* married into my family. Exactly the kind of man."

Five minutes later I was boarding the elevator. "That's a lot of flowers," I said to the man in the blue jumpsuit. "She must really like them."

"It's her disease." he said. "She needs them to cover the odor."

It was something I wish he hadn't told me.

7 "YOU WANT SOME?"

Donna Harris had not only let me in, she'd been happy to see me. She'd put *Ad World* to bed earlier in the evening and was celebrating. Now we were in bed, finished with our lovemaking, watching a John Hodiak mystery on her small Sears black-and-white, and she was offering me some Dannon yogurt.

"Uh-huh," I said.

"Yogurt's good for you." Even in the darkness her hair was very red and she was very pretty.

"Not your kind," I said.

"What's that supposed to mean?"

"What's in there."

"What's *in* there?"

"Now I know I've got you. Whenever you turn my statement into your question, you're doing some number. So what's in there?"

"I just put in a marshmallow."

"What else?"

"Nothing."

"Donna, c'mon."

"You c'mon, Dwyer. I offer you some yogurt and I get the third degree. God."

"So what else did you add besides the marshmallow?"

She sighed, turned around, and faced the TV. It was ghosty again. When we bought the thing the sales lady said that this ultracheapo model sometimes had reception problems in apartment houses due to all the steel in the building framework. We'd taken it as a sales pitch, but it wasn't one. If an ant so much as crawled across the floor the TV set started ghosting out.

"Is that John Hodiak or Betty Hutton?"

"Funny," she said, still pissed.

I leaned over and kissed her. "You really mad?"

"Yes."

"Honey, I've got to watch my waistline. You know that." It was true. Fat guys didn't get many acting jobs in commercials. "I mean, you can get away with eating what you like, but I can't."

She looked at me and sighed and then kissed me on the cheek. "You're right, Dwyer. I was being selfish. You know how some people hate to drink alone? I guess I hate to pig out alone."

"Right. So now will you tell me what you put in there?"

She held it up to the black-and-white glow of the TV set as if we could see into the yogurt with our X-ray vision.

"Well, the marshmallow like I said, and it really was tiny. Then some carob-covered raisins. But just a few."

"Right."

"And then about six Hershey's kisses I had lying around in the cupboard."

"How many is 'about' six?"

"Boy, Dwyer, what an asshole."

"How many?"

"I'm not sure. Maybe a dozen, I guess."

44

"A dozen. God." Her metabolism was phenomenal. She ate pancakes for breakfast, Big Macs for lunch, and Red Lobster specials for dinner and never gained a pound. She worked out three times a week, but not as if she were training to take on the heavyweight champ. I envied her, especially when, as now, we were watching TV and she had a bed full of junk food boxes (exactly what is a "Whanger," anyway?) and was eating enough to feed all the starving orphans in Korea. All I got was my little glass of Pepsi Free.

She finished the yogurt, looking at me occasionally with a demonic gleam in her eyes.

"What're you doing?" she said twenty minutes later.

"Just writing some things down on a clipboard."

"What things?"

"About the case."

"Wade's case? You going to let me see?"

"I guess."

She had one of those tiny lights that clip on to a book to read in bed. She hooked it on the clipboard and read.

"Wow," she said, "we've got some real leads here."

I paid special notice to the "we."

"Nothing real strong, unfortunately."

"The ex-convict named Lockhart talks his way into Reeves's office, obviously looking for something. Keech tries to slap Reeves a few days ago. Evelyn could have known that Reeves was stepping out on her. Anne Stewart was up in Reeves's office tonight. You don't think they're real strong? You're nuts, Dwyer."

"Thanks for the vote of confidence."

"You know what I mean."

"Yeah, I'm nuts."

"I don't have anything to do tomorrow—and you have the day off—so I'll prove it to you," she said.

"Great."

"I can tell you're looking forward to this."

She leaned over and kissed me. The kiss got a lot more serious than I thought it would, but it didn't go anyplace. For the next few minutes we went through our nighttime ritual. I always muttered a few prayers under my breath, and so did she, except she always muttered louder than I did. She must have known what I was doing, and I sure knew what she was doing, but we never once discussed it. Adults with any pretense of hipness should never admit that they pray.

I was asleep in three-and-a-half minutes.

The phone was on my side. I got it.

"Hello," I said.

There was traffic noise in the background. He was obviously calling from an outdoor phone.

"Wade, I know it's you."

Nothing.

"Wade, you really should turn yourself in. You really should."

I felt Donna press against my back. Muzzily, she said, "Let me talk to him, hon." I handed her the phone. "Stephen, listen, please. We love you very much and we're very afraid of what might happen if you don't turn yourself in. Stephen? Do you understand?"

She held the phone out so we could both hear anything he said. What he said was nothing, at least for a long time. Then, "I really fucked it up good this time, didn't I?"

No doubt about it. It was Stephen Wade. Then he hung up.

Five minutes later I was wide awake. Donna, next to me in the darkness, had started to cry softly. "We're going to find out who really killed him, Dwyer. The first goddamn thing tomorrow that's exactly what we're going to do."

She was serious, too.

8 THE HALFWAY HOUSE WHERE THE MAN NAMED
Lockhart was staying was located on the edge of
the city's only acknowledged ghetto. Under the
overcast sky the neighborhood looked even bleaker. Black
teenagers who should have been in school lounged sullenly
in front of a grocery store and watched us pass by.

The house we wanted was a three-story job with a new
shingled roof, a captain's walk, three spires, and a front
porch long enough for the Bears to use for a scrimmage.
Sixty or seventy years ago this place had probably been
some banker's version of Shangri-la. Though the tempera-
ture was only in the low fifties and a damp mist gave the sky
a dusky feel, three men were sitting on the porch in rusty
lawn chairs. They watched Donna approach with special,
and understandable, interest. She had gone trendy today,
heels and designer jeans and a baby-blue sweater that could
make you weep.

There's an air about newly released cons. They're
nervous, as if they're waiting for anything they do to get

them hauled right back into the slam again. These guys were to be pitied. They wanted to look at Donna and they did look at Donna but then they looked away quickly, as if the law were going to show up and beat their brains in. In their view, I suppose, I was the law.

I nodded, trying to make the gesture broad and pleasant. Two of them nodded back. One of them snuck a peek at Donna again. He licked his dry lips, as if somebody had just put a big Thanksgiving dinner down in front of him.

"We'd like to see a man named Lockhart," I said.

The first man, in greasy green work clothes that smelled of car oil, smiled. He had bad teeth. "You ain't the only one. He's been gettin' a lot of calls the past couple days."

"You can't find him?"

Now the second man spoke. He was tall and tubercular. His Adam's apple looked like it weighed twenty-five pounds. His face didn't make sense. He had a sad little mouth and a jackal's eyes. "Oh, everybody knows where he's at."

The third man grinned. "He's up in the attic. The poor sumbitch." He had Elvis sideburns and greasy black hair. Blackheads gave his face an unfinished look, like a board with too many knots. "Anderson's gonna keep him there, too, you can bet your ass on that."

"Anderson the man around here?"

"You got that right, mister," the first one said.

"He inside?"

The third man guffawed. "He always inside, pal. Always. Try'n sneak out some time and you'll find if he's inside or not."

It was then, for the first time, that I realized that these guys were stoned. Between the first and second I saw a small brown prescription bottle. It probably contained cough syrup, which is a cheap high because it doesn't take much and it lasts a long time.

"All right if we go inside?" I asked.

"Hey, prince, you're askin' the wrong man."

I smiled. "Guess we'll have to go inside to find out if it's all right to go inside, huh?" But they were too stoned to see the irony.

We went inside. I almost had to pick their eyeballs off Donna's behind, like ticks after a picnic.

Once there had been a vestibule but it had been knocked out. Now most of the first floor was one big communal room with wobbly furniture from at least five different eras. There was a Motorola black-and-white that had been new about the time Uncle Miltie was laying claim to Tuesday nights, and a phonograph that had probably played a lot of Bing Crosby records. From the kitchen drifted the odors of institutional food: oversalted, oversweetened, anything to kill the taste. There was a residue of cigarette smoke that could have been cut with hedge clippers. It was a sad place, a place where men without women and without dreams passed days in front of the TV or under the thumb of a minimum-wage boss who hated them—men who feared the slammer but didn't really know where else to go. The majority, hapless, hopeless, would be back there within six months.

I took Donna's arm and led her over to a big board that looked like a flight schedule in a terminal. There was a long list of men's names, and next to each was written the place where he was employed. Next to these were two boxes, one that read "Time Out" and one that read "Time Back."

We were reading all this when a whiskey voice behind us said, "Help you folks?"

When he reached us, I saw that his voice complimented his body perfectly. He had slicked-back forties-style hair and a wide, flat Slavic face with black eyes that knew all sorts of truths that most of us would rather not know. He had a gold-capped tooth and he used Aqua Velva green and he put out a hand that could have crushed a whole six-pack of beer. He wore an old blue cardigan sweater that sloped to cover his considerable girth and gray OshKosh washable pants and a pair of leather house slippers that fit as tightly as shoes. He was every boss in every institution I'd ever known.

I introduced myself and Donna, and then he introduced himself as B. J. Anderson. "Mr. Anderson," I said, "we're looking for a man named Lockhart."

He smiled with his gold tooth. "Well, you've come to the right place, but unfortunately you've come at the wrong time. I'm afraid Mr. Lockhart has gone and got himself grounded."

"Do you mind if I ask what for?"

He kept on smiling. "Not if you don't mind if I ask why you're so interested in Mr. Lockhart."

I decided to tell him the truth. "He may know something about a murder."

The smile went back into mothballs. "Lockhart? Murder?"

I explained our association with Wade, and how Stan, the janitor at the theater, had said that Lockhart had come over to look through Reeves's office.

"So that's where he went," B. J. Anderson said.

"Pardon?"

"The other night Lockhart went out past his curfew. When he got back he looked kinda shook up but he wouldn't tell me nothing. Not a goddamn thing. So I put him up in the attic." He raised his black eyes toward the upstairs. "That's where I keep 'em when they've been bad." The smile played on his lips. "This is the only halfway house in the state that hasn't had a man involved in a felony. And you know why? 'Cause I just put the bad apples upstairs and let them cool their heels a little bit."

Donna said, "We'd really like to talk to him if we could."

For the first time he seemed to recognize her. But he was past sex; he had his institution, and that was more fulfilling than any woman had ever been. "I'm not sure that'd be a good idea, miss."

"It's very important."

He turned back to me. "You say you used to be a police officer?"

"Yes."

"You mind if I check that out."

"Not at all." I gave him Edelman's name and extension."

"Be right back."

"Spooky guy," she whispered when he was gone. "No wonder so many men go back to prison. They'd probably do anything to get away from him."

He came back maybe five minutes later and said, "Edelman damned you with faint praise."

"Meaning what?"

"Oh, he said you had been a detective all right, and a decent one, and that you were a trustworthy type, but he didn't seem all that happy that you were spending your time working on this Wade thing." He looked at us and tucked a sour little expression into the corner of his mouth. "Hell, I read all about that Wade character. Alcoholic personality, violent tendancies when he's juiced; hell, folks, our prisons are filled with people like that. Why should some TV star be any exception?"

Donna said, "We'd really like to see Lockhart, Mr. Anderson."

51

He sighed and pushed his hands deep into his Osh-Koshes. "If I tell you five minutes then I mean five minutes, you understand?"

We both nodded like good little children.

He took us up a flight of stairs narrow and twisting enough to be part of one of those horror houses for kids that appear around Halloween. The stairs smelled of dust and disinfectant. When we reached the second floor we saw a large open area with bunk beds. Though there was another TV set and old posters of Farah Fawcett and Racquel Welch in their prime, there was no mistaking what this was. The place smelled of piss and jism and troubled sleep and grief. It was a different kind of prison than the ones the men had been in previously, but it was a prison nonetheless. The gray sky pressed at the window as if to signify as much. Everything in the open area seemed gray.

"It's the next floor we want," Anderson said, and we continued our way up.

By the time we reached the third floor, Anderson, whose fingers were stained mahogany from smoking too many unfiltered cigarettes down too low, had to fall back against the wall to catch his breath.

"I kinda hate puttin' myself through this walk for somebody like that Reeves fella," he said.

"You didn't like him?" I asked.

"Like him?" Anderson said, trying to catch his breath. He looked to be fifty, maybe older. "I hated him. He was a con artist."

"I'm not sure what you mean."

"Those acting classes he came in here and gave for the fellas? Hell, none of them could be actors."

"Keech has done all right," I said. Much as he irritated me sometimes, Keech, the ex-con who played Edmund in *Long Day's Journey Into Night,* was a very good actor.

"Keech might be an exception, yeah."

"You don't like him?"

"He's kind of a pantywaist for my taste."

"Keech?"

"Yeah. He reads too much."

"You don't think reading's good for you?"

"Some reading's very good for you. But Reeves turned him on to all kinds of weird psychology books. Hypnosis, stuff like that. And that's what I mean: that kind of crap shouldn't be made available to cons."

"Why not?"

"Because it just confuses the good ones and they're confused enough. They get a lot of pressure from the bad ones already, believe me." The compassion in his voice surprised me, as did the air of protectiveness. For the first time I found myself liking B.J. Anderson.

"I don't understand where Lockhart fits into all this. Was he in the acting course?" I asked.

"Yeah, unfortunately, he was. He's kind of a pretty-boy type. Easy to flatter. Soon as he met up with Reeves, he became Reeves's errand boy. He'd do anything Reeves asked him. Like in those 'truth' sessions that Reeves liked so much. Lockhart would get real savage with the other guys. He'd force men to admit things about themselves that damn near tore them apart." I could see Reeves doing this. He directed plays in much the same way, keeping his actors hurt and off guard so he could control them absolutely. Being a director was for him a compensation, a substitute for something much darker.

"Well, let's go see Lockhart," Anderson said.

The rest of the walk was down a long, wide corridor. The walls were swollen from moisture. Up this high you could hear the wind. Through a window I saw a greening maple tree.

53

Anderson went to a door that was padlocked from the outside. The padlock was so big it looked comic, like something a circus clown might have.

"Shit," he said.

"What's wrong?"

"Listen."

We listened. "I'm afraid I don't hear anything."

"That's the point. Should be some kind of noise in there."

He took the key, inserted it in the lock, and let us into the room. It was bigger than a prison cell, but less adorned. It had once been a bathroom, apparently. There was a stool, but where the sink had been there were now just two gaping plumbing holes. There was a plastic air mattress on the floor.

"I'll be goddamned and go to hell," B.J. Anderson said as the three of us stared at the floor. The room was empty.

Above was a window with two bars. It was an old story, one that happens in ten jails somewhere in the country every day. The window was smashed. One of the bars had been hacked through with something sharp.

B.J. Anderson said, "Doesn't look like you're going to talk to Mr. Lockhart, after all."

WE ATE AT DENNY'S.

"I could never do that," Donna said over her fish sandwich and fries.

"What?"

"Climb down a three-story wall the way Lockhart did."

"You could if you were desperate enough to get out."

"He must have been very desperate."

"He was."

"He really used a hacksaw?"

"Probably."

"I thought that was only in Heckel and Jeckel cartoons."

"Heckel and Jeckel?"

"Yeah, they were always on the tube when I was a girl. They were always getting out of jail with hacksaws people would bring them inside birthday cakes."

"Gosh," I said, "I'm sorry I missed all those laughs."

"Well, what cartoons did you watch?" She was getting mad.

"The Warner stuff. Bugs Bunny and Elmer Fudd and all those guys. Sylvester."

She said something, but she mumbled it intentionally so I wouldn't hear.

"What?"

She looked as if I'd beaten her at bridge. "I said, 'Yes, the Warner stuff is better than Heckel and Jeckel.'"

"So what're you so pissed about?"

"It just seems weird to me that everything you do is innately superior to everything I do."

"Uh-oh."

"What's that supposed to mean?"

"Just that I was right."

"About what?"

"About what time of month it is."

"God, you keep track?"

"You bet. For reasons of self-defense."

She frowned. "Don't say it, Dwyer. My personality doesn't change when I get my period."

"I couldn't agree more," I said, wanting to avoid our usual argument. I stood up.

"Where are we going?"

"The Bridges Theater. There's something I want to check."

"What?"

"If our friend Keech has ever spent much time with Anne Stewart."

David Ashton was wearing bib overalls with a paint-spotted T-shirt underneath. He was standing on a ladder painting with a wide brush and humming along to a beautiful-music radio station.

"David?"

He looked down from the flat he was painting and nodded to us. "Give me a minute."

Donna walked around and looked at the set for *Long*

Day's Journey. It was very well done, as were most things at the Bridges Theater.

By the time David came down from the ladder, it was apparent from his gaze that he still remembered being humiliated in front of me by his mother-in-law.

"That was quite a little scene last night," he said. "You looked really distressed by it. I just wanted to tell you that I'm used to it by now."

"I told her what I thought about it."

"I wish I could say it would do some good. She still sees me as the interloper. Connived to win myself a fortune and succeeded."

I smiled. "Seems the painting helps you forget. I heard you humming."

"Oh, yes. My two brothers are painters." He looked melancholy for a moment. "The closer I get to fifty, the more I wonder if I shouldn't have spent my life as a laboring man. I mean, after acting didn't work out." He glanced at Donna. "Well, you look beautiful as ever."

"Thanks."

"You two come to take me to lunch?" he laughed.

"Afraid not. I needed to ask you a question."

"Oh? There isn't any more news on Wade, is there?"

"None that I know of."

"The poor bastard. Michael really was insufferable."

"I wanted to ask you about Anne."

"Anne?" He went over and turned the radio off. He looked like a blue-collar man ready for a big lunch. That sort of life seemed to make him happier than running the theater, where he always looked tense. "Nothing's happened to her, has it?"

"No, but something did happen to a man named Lockhart."

"The man who was here the other day?"

"Yes."

I explained what had happened at the halfway house.

"My God. You think it has any connection to Michael's death?"

"I do," I said. "But I'm not sure the police will. At least not at this point." I had decided against telling him why I was suspicious of Anne, so I said, "Have you ever seen Keech and Anne spending any time together?"

He thought a moment. "No, not really. Except during rehearsals they might have had a cup of coffee together. You know how Keech is. If there's a woman, he has to flirt with her. I know he tried coming on to Evelyn right in front of Michael. Michael got very upset."

I thought of Keech trying to hit Michael the other night in the parking lot. Could that have been over Evelyn?

"But nothing between Anne and Keech, no," David said.

We were standing just behind a flat. We couldn't see the east wing, so when somebody bumped against a chair, I couldn't see who it was. But I had a feeling that somebody might have been standing there listening for some time.

I walked around the flat. It was Evelyn.

"Sorry to interrupt you," she said.

David and Donna came around.

"Hello, hon," David said. She came over and let him kiss her. Apparently they'd made up from last night. But maybe not entirely. As usual, David handled his daughter with a certain unease.

"I just wondered if I could borrow your car," she said.

"Sure," David said. "The keys are in my sport coat in the office."

"Thanks." She stood on tiptoes and kissed him on the cheek.

Then she turned to me. "They haven't found Wade, have they?"

"Not yet," I said.

She looked at me frankly. "I hope they take him without hurting him."

Her attitude puzzled me. Wade had supposedly killed her lover. For the first time I began to wonder about Evelyn.

"Well," she said, "see you." She nodded and was gone.

Quickly, I said to Ashton, "Well, David, thanks for the information."

"Afraid I wasn't much help."

"Thanks again."

I took Donna by the elbow. We were in the parking lot within two minutes. I fired up the Honda, whipped around the corner of the lot, and sat there with the engine running.

"I feel confident that you're going to tell me what the fuck is going on, Dwyer."

"Evelyn."

"Gee, that's a good clue. 'Evelyn.' What about Evelyn?"

Ordinarily, Donna would accept the mystery a bit more gracefully than this. I dropped all the coy stuff.

"Say somebody shot me. Wouldn't you be pretty angry with him?"

"Not necessarily."

"Very funny."

"So what's that got to do with Evelyn?"

"Well, she's very bland when the subject of Wade comes up—yet he's the one who everybody thinks killed her lover, Michael."

"Yeah, I guess that sort of makes sense. But I still don't understand why we're parked here."

"We're going to follow her."

"Evelyn."

"Right."

"God, Dwyer, if I didn't have to think about poor Stephen out there somewhere, this would be a lot of fun. It really would."

I patted her hand. "I'm happy for you."

TEN MINUTES LATER, DONNA SAID, "AREN'T you supposed to stay a few blocks back?"

"Where'd you get that idea?"

"I saw it on *Magnum P.I.* one night."

"Oh, right, *Magnum P.I.*"

"Is there something wrong with that show?"

"Not at all," I said. "As a matter of fact, in order to become a policeman in this city you have to watch a minimum of thirty-two episodes."

"Har-de-har-har."

Not that I had any idea where Evelyn Ashton was taking us. In fact, I got the impression after twenty minutes that she might have caught on to us and just be leading us around in circles to frustrate us.

By now Donna was curled up next to the door, asleep. Her period, all jokes aside, came hard and was very difficult for her. I reached over and touched her hip. At times such as these I loved her so much and so purely that it scared my ass off.

Ahead, Evelyn Ashton stayed on her inexplicable course. We went past the city's largest and most exclusive country club; past three blocks of new condos; past a city park where ducks walked around in the mist, looking cute and solemn at the same time; past a burgeoning new area of plastic Holiday Inns and Motel 8s; and then past innumerable FOR SALE signs as we headed for the city limits and wide open spaces.

Finally, I figured out where she was taking us. Out of town, of course. I looked at my gas gauge. Given my usual state of finances, and because I never really left high school, I normally put in five bucks at a time. Fortunately, I'd only recently put in my latest geyser so the Honda could go for many miles.

You could see the spring coming up, even in the rain, which was increasing. There were corn and sorghum and oats and barley in the fields. In the murk, the foliage on the hills ringing the city was dark gray. A farmer on a tractor with bug-eyed headlights waved to us from the other lane. Now that she was on a two-lane highway, Evelyn Ashton seemed not only to know exactly where she was going but also to be in a hell of a hurry to get there.

We went deeper into the country, which was all right with me. I don't like country music, hunting, horseshoes, or barn dances, but I do like living in a city that's no more than twenty minutes away from the countryside. There's a sanity in nature you could never find in the city.

The downpour continued, banging against the roof like bullets.

Donna woke up, reached over, and touched me affectionately on the arm. "How you doing, hon?"

"Fine."

"We still following Evelyn?"

"Yeah." The sleep had mellowed her out.

"We know where she's going yet?"

"Uh-huh."

Donna rubbed some of the steam off the window. "Boy, look at those poor cows."

About a dozen milk cows stood on the side of a bare hill in the rain.

"Yeah," I said, knowing what she meant. I wanted to buy a bunch of rain ponchos and go out there and cover them up.

"Can I turn on the radio?"

"Sure."

"All right if I play Top Forty?"

"Fine." Sometimes jazz bummed her out. Today she didn't need any help being bummed out. A happy tune came on, bright, quick, empty. It was fine with me.

We had now gone maybe twenty miles. Ahead was a small town. Back at the turn of the century there'd been a railroad watering stop here, just big enough for a hamlet of a couple of thousand to spring up. It was named Brackett.

Evelyn turned off the highway on to an asphalt road that led to the town. From there I could see a billboard touting a restaurant that specialized in roast beef dinners. I could also see a DX gasoline sign, a church steeple, and a water tower.

"Damn," I said.

"What?"

"She just turned but I'm not sure where."

Ahead of me, Evelyn had followed the curving road into town. I'd made the mistake of thinking that she would follow the asphalt directly into Brackett. But now that I looked I didn't see her. There were two gravel roads on either side of the asphalt, but they were mostly hidden by blooming trees. She could have turned onto either one.

I'd lost her.

I pounded the steering wheel and said, "Damn it."

"Maybe you should start watching *Magnum P.I.*" She had grace enough to lean over and kiss me.

I took the gravel road that headed east. It ran parallel to a narrow muddy river. Even in the rain there was a fisherman out there in rubber gear in his beat-up boat. He waved. We waved back.

"That's what I like about the country," Donna said. "Everybody's so friendly."

"I'll take you to a small-town bar where the farmhands get together on Friday night," I said, remembering a brawl I'd helped break up one night. "Then you'll see just how friendly the country can get."

"That's it," she said, "spoil my fantasy. Don't you believe in Ibsen's theory?"

"What theory?"

"Boy, Dwyer. You're supposed to be an actor."

"Last month I had to get inside a lumpy brown suit for a commercial and play a potato. I don't know from Ibsen, believe me."

"Well, he had this theory about the 'saving lie.' How the only thing that saves us from cracking up is our delusions."

For some reason, that reminded me of the old woman last night, Mrs. Bridges. Was I trying to save her delusions by clearing the theater of any wrongdoing in Michael Reeves's murder?

For the next few minutes I watched the road. The rain was ceaseless, dismal. Donna twisted herself into a half-foetal and pushed her face to the window to stare out at the dying day. It was one of those times when she looked very much like a little girl. I wanted to hug her.

There was a steep dip in the gravel road, and just below

the crest a small log cabin set between two towering pines appeared.

"Boy, it's like the Old West."

"Yeah, maybe Gabby Hayes is in there."

"Or Wyatt Earp—what's his name, the actor who played him? Boy, was he cute."

The owner of the cabin had made no concession to modern times. There was no place for a car to be parked. There was just a steep clay cliff where the road ended and a wide patch of dead grass where you could take a leak or put your car. I parked.

"Where you going? It's raining," Donna said as I opened the door.

"See who's around."

"Well, obviously Evelyn isn't here. She must've taken the other road."

"I know, but maybe the people inside know something about the territory. Evelyn was obviously going someplace she was familiar with. Which gives her a distinct advantage. Okay?"

"Okay," she said, "then I'll go with you."

The run through the rain was like a trip through a carwash without a car. We got to the little overhang above the door. The air was tangy. It was nice to be dry for the moment and have our senses filled with the smell of pine.

Donna did the knocking. "Man, that stuff is hard on the old knuckles." The door was scaley with bark. There was a faded flour-sack curtain on the lone window. It moved almost imperceptibly. I sensed eyes on us.

"Whaddaya want?" somebody shouted through the logs that formed the wall. It was like putting your lips to your arm and talking.

"Just need some information," I said.

I didn't know where to put my eyes or aim my voice.

"What kinda information?"

"Tell him you'd like to know the meaning of life," Donna said.

"Just some information on the land around here." I was starting to shout.

"You with the press?"

"No."

"Hold on then."

"This guy better be worth the wait," I said. And he almost was.

When the door was flung back a minute or so later, a fifty-year-old man with enough physical eccentricities to be a pro wrestler stood before us, hands on his hips and a scowl on his lips.

He had one burning blue eye; a black patch covered the other. He had fleshy, muscular arms covered with enough tattoos to fill an Oriental sampler. His shirtless torso had knockers big enough to rival a porn star's. His jeans were held up with a piece of honest-to-god twine. In case we hadn't gotten the picture yet, behind him, right in the middle of the single-room cabin, sat a big old Harley with handlebars nearly wide enough to touch either wall and enough chrome to blind you on a sunny day.

"I'm Jake."

"I'm Jack."

"Who's the babe?"

"I'm Donna."

"Jack and Donna, Jake is glad to meet ya."

And he put out a hand you could have rested a typewriter in. Donna did a much better job of disguising the pain his handshake inflicted than I did. She just bit her lip till tears came to her eyes.

We were close enough to Jake that when he raised his arm to proffer the shake, we got a good, if unwanted, look at the splendiferous black hair of his armpits. I mean this bastard could have taken his pits on tour. I've seen less hair in full beards.

But there was a problem with his pits, as there was a problem with his place. To say it smelled like a pig sty would be to understate. It was one of those high, hard odors that made you wince and then shudder and then cup your nose. (I used to have an uncle who should have put a flashing red light on the bathroom door for an hour after he was finished in there.)

"You wanna come inside?" Jake asked.

"No," I said.

"No, we like it out here in the cold rain," Donna said.

"She kiddin' or what?" Jake said.

"No, cold and rain are two of her favorite things. Put them together and she goes bug shit."

"Weird broad," Jake said.

"Isn't she, though," I said. I was going to pay for that one. "Can I ask you a question, Jake?"

"Sure." For a moment, he sounded like a pirate. I almost expected him to add, "Matey." He smiled, giving us a look at a set of teeth that could have tired out a full team of dentists.

"Why did you want to know if we were with the press?"

"Aww, hell, the election."

"Election? It's May."

"No, the Road Knights's election."

"Road Knights?"

He flung a flabby arm toward the Harley. "I'm the president of the Knights, you know. But this is the first year in thirty fucking—excuse me, lady—years I've got some-body runnin' against me."

"The Road Knights are a biker gang and the press covers your election?"

"Well, maybe 'press' is stretchin' things a bit. It's actually just a guy named Schleimer who runs the local county shopper. He says there's a lot of interest about the Knights 'cause we're always gettin' in so much trouble with the law'n all and folks'll be curious about the election. So I'm just sittin' it out here today while all the ballots are cast at the tavern in Brackett."

"Think you're gonna win?"

He made a fist. Hell, I was impressed. "I goddamn better."

"Democracy in action," Donna said. I wanted to turn around and say to her, okay, if you're so frigging smart why don't you let *me* hide behind *you* and then wise off to him? Jake didn't catch her exact meaning, but he knew a smartass when he saw one.

"Actually, Jake, we're wondering if a car came past here within the last few minutes."

He opened his mouth very wide and threw his head back and laughed. These days everybody is an actor. "A car came past here? Where the hell would it go? Through the cliff over there?" He threw his head back again and did some more laughing. Maybe he thought I was a mobile Equity man and could give him his card on the spot.

"We were coming down the asphalt into Brackett and we noticed two gravel roads. We took this one. You know what's on the other one?"

"Dead end, just like this one."

"There a cabin there or anything?"

"Yeah. But not a cabin like this one. Big fancy-ass one is what it is. The Knights tried to bust in there one night but then the doctor showed up. In these parts nobody wants to fuck with the doctor." When he cursed, he glanced at Donna as if she might lob a hot brick at him.

"Who's the doctor?"

"Guy name of Kern."

"He live in the cabin?"

"No, he lives next to his funny farm."

"A mental hospital?"

"Yeah, but that ain't what they call it. You know, it's like the Sunrise Retreat or somethin' like that. But it's still for nut cases. You know, psychos and fags and intellectuals."

I could see that Donna was getting ready to laugh. I hoped she didn't. My jaw was still a lot closer to his fist than hers was.

"But he stays at the cabin sometimes?"

"Yeah. Even takes some of those fruitcakes along with him sometimes." He shook his head in solid-citizen disgust. "The fucking people they let run loose, it makes you wonder, just like my old man always said; it just goddamn makes you wonder."

She couldn't take it any more, Donna couldn't. She knew that if she laughed Jake here would put me to the wall. So she started to wave us off (as if a runner on third were about to steal home) and at the same time to back out into the rain.

I tried to distract him from watching her by keeping my questions going. "So how long has Doctor Kern owned the cabin?"

"Oh, he don't own it, Kern don't. It belongs to some rich-ass friends of his."

"Who's that?"

"City friends of his. The Bridges family."

Donna, who was still backing out into the rain, stopped. "The Bridges family?"

He looked at her. "Yeah. I say something wrong?"

She shook her head.

"How come she's standin' in the rain?" he asked me.

"Cold and rain, remember?" I said. "Two of her favorite things." I got another whiff of the cabin. It was like flashing on your own death. "Well, gee, Jake, I sure hope you win that election."

He raised his fist again. "Don't you worry about that. Like I told Schleimer at the shopper, I'm gonna win one way or the other."

Behind me, in the gloom, the car door closed. Even from where I stood I heard Donna burst out laughing. Thankfully, Jake didn't seem to notice.

He put out his hand again. I didn't have any choice. I said a Hail Mary and put out my hand, too. If things didn't go Jake's way in the election, he could hire out as a trash compactor.

"He was a reasonably nice guy," I said as I got the car started.

"Right."

"Well, he was civil."

"Oh, that's right, Dwyer. Maybe that's why he reminded me so much of St. Francis of Assissi. Here all the time I thought it was his bike. You know, St. Francis had a Harley just like Jake's."

"You're a snob."

She finally quit laughing and said, "No, I'm not. I just don't like bullies."

"He wasn't a bully."

"Maybe not right now, he wasn't. But I've had a number of bad experiences with bikers pulling into picnic grounds and onto beaches. They travel in packs because they want to intimidate people and that's the only reason."

This was one argument she was definitely winning. I changed the subject. "So the Bridges own the other cabin."

"Which would explain why Evelyn knew exactly where she was going. Grandma's."

We were coming up to the asphalt road. The rain was

drumming now. The wipers slowed perceptibly under the weight.

We got on the asphalt and drove the two hundred yards to the gravel road running west. That's when we saw Evelyn's car.

It shot past the final yards of pines fronting the gravel road, heading for the asphalt. She hit the main road hard enough that her whole car jerked when her front wheels hit the smooth surface. But she didn't stop, nor did she look in either direction for oncoming cars. Obviously she was badly upset about something. She just swung the car onto the asphalt and started heading our way.

"Look," Donna said, leaning up to the windshield so she could see through the downpour, "she's got somebody with her."

Indeed she did. I had to look through the mosaic of raindrops to make sure that my first impulse had been correct—that I was seeing who I thought I was seeing. As their car roared toward us, I knew for sure.

Her passenger was the mysterious Keech, my fellow actor in the O'Neill play.

I wondered if Evelyn Ashton knew what kind of company she was keeping. Or cared.

"Are we going to follow them?" Donna asked, excited at the prospect.

"I think we'd better check out the cabin," I said. "They must've found something back there."

She shot me one of her looks. "You really don't watch *Magnum, P.I.*, do you?"

JAKE'S CABIN COULD HAVE SERVED AS A GARDEN shed for the Bridges cabin. Two-storied, with a barn-style roof, the place looked like a small resort hotel, complete with a U-shaped drive that curved right up to the long porch. It was the only "cabin" I'd ever seen with mullioned windows.

"Just a nice little lean-to," Donna said.

"Maybe if Jake wins the election, they'll let him move in here."

She laughed as we got out of the car. Then she waved for me to take her hand for the run to the cabin. The rain was cold and blinding. The ground was soggy enough to pull you down like quicksand.

"Boy, I'll bet it's beautiful out here when the weather's nice," Donna said when we'd reached the porch and were safe under the overhang.

She was right. Several hundred yards ahead of us was the river, lined with weeping willows. On the distant shore were steep hills and an impenetrable forest of pines. It was almost like being in the mountains. We turned back to the front door.

Now there was a man standing there. A tall, gray-haired man in a three-piece suit. He might have been a bank president in a TV commercial. Except for the shotgun in his arms. That was a very inappropriate prop for a bank president to be carrying.

Cabins in this area seemed to be inhabited by some really strange people.

He pulled the inner door open and said, "May I help you?"

"Is there a reason for the shotgun?" I asked.

"Unless you're illiterate, you read several signs on the road leading here. They each say NO TRESPASSING. That's the reason for the shotgun."

Now that I could see him more clearly, I saw that he had a patrician face that had turned a bit jowly. He was in his early sixties or so. He had clear blue eyes that curiously held no expression, almost like a doll's. I assumed that he was Dr. Kern, the guy whom Leonora Bridges had referred to as "a family friend" and the man the biker had said everybody was afraid of.

"I'm Jack Dwyer," I said. "This is Donna Harris."

He nodded. "My name is Dr. Kern."

I tried to avoid Donna's eyes when he said that. She's got this Eureka! look that sometimes tips our hand.

"We don't mean to trespass, Dr. Kern," I said. "I guess we just kind of got lost in the rain."

He nodded. He looked sad. The shotgun he held suddenly looked ineffectual. He didn't scare me anymore. He just made me curious.

"So is there some way I can help you?" he asked.

I wasn't sure what I was going to say next. Donna, with

great charm and even greater conviction, said, "We only stopped because I need to use a restroom."

"Oh, of course," he said. He indicated for us to come inside and pointed out the bathroom to her.

The interior smelled sweetly of log smoke. The rain on the roof made everything feel cozy and safe, with the big fieldstone fireplace, the rows of bookcases with a few hundred hardcovers, the simple elegance of the leather furniture. There was a TV set as big as my Civic and a dining table next to a huge stained-glass window. The table looked like it could seat about twenty people. A bouquet of red paper roses looked lonely on the long table.

"You're from the city?" he inquired.

"Yes."

He went over and laid the shotgun down on a desk. "I apologize again for the gun. The way things are these days . . . well, you understand."

"Of course."

He saw where my eyes had rested. His mouth. The blood.

"Oh, I banged myself on a door," he said, daubing at the red stuff.

I smiled. I hope I looked sincere. He seemed a decent enough guy.

"Do you live here?"

"Oh, no," he said, "I only bring some of my patients here occasionally. I have a clinic about a mile from here."

"I see."

"The patients appreciate getting out. In good weather, this is a very nice environment."

"It certainly is."

We both glanced up the long stairs. I wondered if Donna had taken a couple of magazines in there with her. The doctor and I were fast running out of things to talk about. I was wondering if I was going to ask about the migration habits of squirrels when Donna appeared again. To me it was obvious that she was excited about something.

"Thank you very much," she said to Dr. Kern.

"Not at all. And, as I was saying to Mr. Dwyer, I do apologize about the shotgun. We've had vandals lately."

"I understand," Donna said.

He smiled at her. She was easy to smile at even though she was six feet tall and could eat your meal *and* hers in three minutes flat.

He walked us to the door. We said our good-byes again and we ran to the car.

Inside, Donna said, "Boy, did I find some things out upstairs."

"Like what?"

"Like somebody went through several of the rooms up there and turned everything inside out. Looks like a bomb hit it."

I started the car and pulled away.

"Aren't we going to check it out, Dwyer?" she asked as I headed down the road.

"Yeah. But we've got to find someplace to hide until we see the doctor leave."

"Oh, yeah, right. Good thinking." She had the pure enthusiasm of a sixteen-year-old.

"So I just told Chad to leave me alone. I mean, there wasn't much he could say after he handed me a ring and I led him into the bathroom and made him watch me flush it down the toilet."

The subject was Chad, her ex-husband.

A few months ago she'd gone to Mexico on a lonely vacation to forget him. I'd been skeptical about the results, but apparently it had worked. Oh, Chad, who had dumped her for a younger woman and had then changed his mind, Chad was still around, calling her more frequently than her mother, making the sorts of promises that only somebody who has the looks of Robert Redford and the personality of John Davidson can make. She genuinely seemed to be working him out of her life. Lately, I'd even felt some pity for the bastard. I don't really wish heartbreak on anybody. I was there once myself. I lost thirty pounds and more than a little dignity.

"So he hasn't called for nearly a whole week," she said.

"Gosh. Ma Bell must be getting nervous."

"God, Dwyer, look."

A black Buick, the sort of car monsignors always drove back in the era of Bishop Sheen, came up to the asphalt, paused, and then proceeded north.

We sat with the motor off in a grove of white birches just off the highway. If Dr. Kern saw us, he didn't let on.

"Great," she said, "now we can go back to the cabin."

We stood in the open area in front of the fireplace, looking around. The place still smelled sweetly of log smoke. The leather furniture needed dusting, the kitchen sink contained some unwashed dishes, and sections of the bookcases needed straightening. But all the same I'd have lived there if they asked me. The freezer alone, over in the kitchen area, must have cost more than my Honda. You could have gotten several head of cattle in it. Live ones.

"You want to start upstairs?" Donna said.

"Sure. Why not?"

She looked at me. "Boy, Dwyer, you don't seem very up."

"Three days of rain. It's starting to get to me."

Then she said, quite seriously, "You're being selfish. I've never seen you be selfish before." She leaned over and kissed me tenderly on the mouth. "Think of Wade out there. Think what he must be going through. He's not sure if he's a murderer or not. We have to help him."

I followed her, pretty much down on myself (so it's raining, big fucking deal; the homeless and hungry and malformed of the world probably have it a bit tougher than I do). When we came to the top of the stairs, Donna stopped and peered into a large denlike room and said, "He cleaned it up."

I glanced in. "This was the room that was tossed?"

She nodded.

"No wonder he had the shotgun," I said. "He probably figured we were the vandals coming back for a second round."

She led the way inside.

"You think we should look around?" she said.

"Wouldn't hurt."

She gave me a half-scowl. "C'mon, Dwyer, you still sound morose."

I put on a fake cheesy smile. "Gee, Donna, I'd love to search this room."

"That's better."

"Up yours."

"I heard that."

"I meant for you to hear that."

"What an asshole."

We set to work. The first twenty minutes I found nothing interesting. Medical journals filled some drawers; shirts, socks, and underwear filled others. The daybed in the corner, covered with a spread and tossed with colorful pillows, was apparently where Dr. Kern slept. That made sense; the other rooms all had bunk beds, for patients, I assumed.

Then Donna said, "Boy, Dwyer, come over here."

At the end of the daybed was a big wicker trunk. She had the lid up and was stacking stuff on the floor.

I knelt next to her, pecking her on the cheek as I did so.

What she was setting out for me to see was three decades of Dr. Kern's history at the sanitarium and here at the cabin. He seemed to feel a true fondness for his patients. The floor was covered with photographs of Dr. Kern at various ages, standing in the midst of grinning groups of people. Most of the photos had been taken in front of the cabin here. The patients looked happy, if a bit distant; presumably they were taking some kind of medication. The clothes they wore recalled their eras exactly, from the silky, feminine print dresses of the late forties (women never looked more like women than in the late forties and early fifties) to the dull pants suits of the seventies. Here was Kern as a young man with thick glasses, a pipe, and a mop of hair that gave him the air of an engineer; a decade or so later his hair was parted, his glasses were horn-rimmed, and he wore a tan workshirt that lent him the look of an archeologist on a distant dig. Only a few years later, he seemed to have aged and become the man he was today, fleshy and benign and bankerly, the eyes oddly vacant of meaning, as if they only perceived and did not judge what they saw. When he was surrounded by grateful patients, he looked happy and competent. But when he was alone—as in the picture that showed him leaning against the door of a 1957 DeSoto—he seemed vulnerable in the way that only a big man can, and more than a bit lost. He might have been a child waiting for his mother after school.

"Look at this," Donna said. She showed me a piece of parchment. It was Kern's M.A.M.D. diploma. He was a bona fide shrink—a medical doctor first, a psychiatrist second. He had become a doctor in 1948. The diploma had been issued from one of the state universities.

"But these are the weird things," she said. She handed me some playbills from the Bridges Theater dating back to the early sixties. Even then some of the stars they'd attracted were big names. Dale Robertson, Keefe Brasselle, Liz Scott, and Donald O'Connor had been among the guest actors. "I wonder why he'd keep those."

I shrugged. "Don't know. Unless he has an interest in theater, too." I looked at the whole stack. They were printed on very glossy paper, faded somewhat now to a yellow-gray. The hairstyles were out of date. O'Connor looked seventy pounds lighter. I kept going through the playbills, which were all pretty much alike, and then I set them down again. Sometimes I'm sort of suffused with understanding of how time passes—how it's a rush unfolding infinitely from one end of eternity to the other and how our lives aren't so much as a micro-second in the roar of its passage. Then it's better to force myself to think of something else, and fast.

"Wow," Donna said, laughing. "Here are some really strange playbills."

These were of people more familiar. On the front of one playbill could be seen Wade and Sylvia and David Ashton. They all looked impossibly young and attractive and arrogant. They starred in Noel Coward's *Private Lives*.

"Sylvia was really a beauty," I said.

"Well, Wade wasn't so bad himself," Donna said with an edge, and I remembered her jealousy.

"Christ, I didn't mean anything by it. I just meant that she was very attractive before she started having her breakdowns."

"Yeah, but it was the way you said it. You haven't sounded enthusiastic about anything all day, and then you see this old photo of Sylvia and you really get enthusiastic. How would you feel?"

"I don't get jealous as easily as you do."

"Don't get jealous? God, Dwyer, if you really believe that then *you* should see Kern."

"I thought we were gathering evidence here to help out Wade." But I knew her and knew what she was like when she got mad.

"How about the other night in the pizza place?"

I felt myself flush. I'd thought my reaction had been noticeable only to myself. "What pizza place?"

She mocked me. "'What pizza place?' The one where the blond guy named Kevin came up. The guy I used to date? The guy who kept telling me how great I looked and didn't seem to notice you there at all?"

"Oh, yeah," I said, "that pizza place."

"Right. That pizza place."

"What about it?"

"What about it? Are you crazy? You were so jealous you hardly spoke to me for about three hours afterwards, and when I invited you in, you said you had a headache." She shook her red hair. "A headache. Boy, Dwyer, I expected more of you than that."

"I had a headache. No big deal."

"The big deal is, Dwyer, that I can admit I'm the jealous type and you can't."

"It's because I'm not."

"You're blushing, Dwyer."

"Bullshit."

"Bullshit. You—are—blushing. And you know why? Because you're telling a lie."

Just as she said that, two things happened. The playbills fell out of my hands and I saw the bill that featured David Ashton alone on it. I was starting to reach for it when the second thing happened—downstairs, out in the rain, a car door slammed.

"Somebody's here," I said.

But her temper was not to be put off. She grabbed my sleeve. "I won't let you do anything until you admit it."

"Admit what?"

She made one of those faces that one pro wrestler makes to another just before he's going to put the Mongolian Motherfucker on the poor guy. Except in Donna's case, she was serious. She grabbed my sleeve and twisted it. "Admit that you get jealous just like I do."

Then I heard a second car door slam.

"Okay," I said, "I'll admit it, but only because somebody's coming."

The Mongolian Motherfucker expression had yet to leave her face. "You're going to pay for this, Dwyer. I promise you."

I stuffed the playbill with David Ashton into the pocket of my sport coat and jumped to the window.

"This is really getting crazy," I said.

"Who is it?" She'd calmed down enough to get interested in investigation again.

"Anne Stewart and her husband."

"What are they doing here?"

I shrugged. "We're about to find out." I looked around for someplace to hide. The only place I could find was the walk-in closet in the next room. "You coming in?" I called, hearing the doorbell bong downstairs.

"You going to admit you get jealous?"

"All right for God's sake, I admit it."

"Good. That time you sounded serious."

I reached out and pulled her in and pushed us both down into the gloom at the back of the closet. Then I leaned up and slid the doors closed.

"Now what?" Donna said.

Right after she said it, we heard the glass in the door

break downstairs. Anne Stewart and her husband seemed very anxious to get in for some reason. Because we'd parked in the deep forest behind the cabin, well out of sight, the Stewarts would naturally assume the place was empty.

There was another sound of shattering glass, the door creaked open, and we heard tramping feet. The Stewarts were inside.

12 FOR A LONG TIME WE HEARD NOTHING. JUST our breathing in the closeness of the closet.

Then a chair scraped downstairs; doors were jerked open, banged shut. Above us rain hammered the roof. I could smell strawberry jam on Donna's breath; her stomach gurgled symphonically several times (she's got the only stomach I know that can do arias). Then more chairs scraping, more doors being jerked open and banging shut.

The stairway creaked. The Stewarts were on their way up.

Donna's nails bit into my wrist. She whispered, "What if they find us in here?"

I whispered back. "If we keep whispering, they damn well will."

She took great offense. "Oh. Sorry." Her nails withdrew. "I don't suppose I'm behaving like a professional detective, am I?"

She scooched away from me, as far to the other side of the closet as possible.

Wonderful.

At the top of the stairs, Anne Stewart said, "I suppose we should split up and start checking rooms." I thought of Anne sneaking out of Michael Reeves's office at the theater. Whatever she'd been looking for was obviously still unfound.

"This is a great way to spend a day." Her husband's voice was harsh and carried more than a hint of bitterness. I'd met Donald once. He was a short, trim man who divided his life between the white smock of dentistry and the blue togs of Adidas. At fifty, he was apparently a marathoner of some repute.

Anne said, "Maybe you should wait in the car."

"Maybe I should go see my lawyer."

"That's up to you, Donald. All I care about is that you give up your whining."

"Maybe I could if I could get a certain image out of my mind. You on his bed with your legs spread—"

"Goddamn you!" The slap was gunshot sharp. In the silence afterwards were unspoken rage and the rain.

Then there were tears. She musn't have been practiced at crying, Anne Stewart, because she more choked than sobbed.

"Can't you at least fucking hold me?" she said after a time. Now it was her turn for bitterness. "I'm your wife."

"You only seem to remember that when it's convenient."

She started choking again. Finally tears came pure. She sounded almost like a little girl. He let her cry. Maybe he thought letting her cry was good for her. Or maybe he hated her so much he couldn't bring himself to touch her.

In the darkness, Donna's hand found mine and squeezed.

The gesture told me what she was feeling. A terrible kind of awe in the face of two human beings destroying each other.

"I'll try this room first," Donald Stewart said as his wife's tears began to subside.

"Wait. I want to say something."

"We've said it fucking all," Donald said. The anger was back in his voice. There was weariness there now, too.

"I never for a moment loved him. I wasn't unfaithful in that way."

"No, you just let him screw your brains out."

Pity shook him, but you knew right away it was for himself and not for any notion of them as a couple. "I wish I could get somebody to cut the thoughts I have out of my brain. I mean that, Anne. Just cut them out like a cancer so that I didn't know that you'd slept with him and didn't know that you wrote him those letters—"

"It hasn't been easy for me. You've changed—ever since you started embezzling." She meant to hurt him and obviously she had. He was silent.

"But why did you have you tell Reeves about it?" he said after a time, miserably.

"Let's just see if the letters are here someplace and not talk," Anne said. "I'm so damn tired of talking."

They searched for half an hour and made a great deal of noise. A couple of times they called out to each other as if something important had been discovered, but in the end they didn't seem to find anything. They finished back at the top of the stairs again.

"Great, just fucking great," Donald said.

"Maybe we can try his apartment tonight."

"That's one I'll let you handle yourself. I'm really not up for seeing the bed where you let him turn you into a whore."

They went down the stairs and across the hardwood floor and outside, dragging their griefs along behind them.

Car doors opened and slammed. A transmission whined in reverse. The sound of the motor was lost on the vanishing point of rain.

The weird thing was, we didn't move. Even long after it was all right to crawl out of the closet and begin to bring proper circulation back to our legs and buttocks, we sat there and just listened to the rain.

"We shouldn't argue," Donna said.

"Yeah. I know."

"After hearing them, loving somebody sounds so hopeless."

She came into my arms. We didn't kiss. We just held each other. "It's so fucking scary," she said.

"Yeah," I said, "yeah it is."

We never did kiss there, just held each other (I kept my eyes closed and smelled her hair and skin, the soft warmth of them) and then we went downstairs and got into our car and drove off.

As soon as I got back into town, I pulled up to an outdoor phone and called the American Security office. Just before they answered I started hacking suddenly.

"God, are you all right?" Donna asked.

I turned my back into the receiver and really blasted it down the phone lines.

"Bobby Lee?" I said between blasts.

"Are you all right, Dwyer?" Bobby Lee said.

I should tell you about her. She is an amply endowed lady who wears Merle Haggard T-shirts and a beehive hairdo you could hide microwaves inside. She buys pro wrestling magazines, and is also the receptionist where I work. She was also the receptionist at our previous place of employment, where she had another duty as well—mistress to the owner. When the man threw her out, she rediscovered the wisdom of the most fundamentalist Baptist church in the city and has since given up swearing, married men, and, alas, her tighter T-shirts. Her new man is Harold, a wholesale auto parts dealer. He's also a born-again Republican who genuinely believes that Latin America is ours to do with as we see fit, and the bass in a barbershop quartet. Whether you choose to believe it or not, he's also a gentle, intelligent, and warm man and I'm damn glad Bobby Lee found him, for both their sakes.

"Just picked up a cold," I said. "I'd better talk to Kastle."

But Bobby Lee, who still appreciated my getting her this job, said, "Let me handle it, Dwyer. I'm going to tell him you're sick and need to be in bed for at least a day. Now you just tell Donna to fix you up some soup and head for bed. You understand me?"

I gave her another blast for good measure. "Well, if you say so."

"Soup and bed, Dwyer, and no ifs, ands, or buts—all right?"

"All right," I said between hacks.

After I hung up, Donna said, "Boy, I don't know if I'll ever believe anything you tell me after that performance."

"I'm sure I'm going to need the day off tomorrow. We're getting close to something."

"Yes, but what?"

"I'm not sure. Now I'm going to call the answering service and then we're going over to Reeves's."

"Why Reeves's?"

"Because that's who Anne and her husband had to be talking about." I reminded her about seeing Anne come out of Reeves's office. "Maybe we'll turn something up. We can also ask the tenants some questions." I searched in my pockets. Nothing. There was a clap of thunder. The rain came down even harder. I felt wet and cold. I wanted to be under a warm electric blanket. "You got two dimes?"

She looked in her purse. She had two dimes. I called my answering service. The people who had called me included my agent, my insurance man, a costume rental place I still owed twenty bucks, and a Mr. Tyrone, who said he'd meet me tonight at St. Philomena's at 9:00 P.M. I thanked her and hung up.

"We're going to see Wade tonight," I said as we pulled away.

"How do you know?"

"He left word with my service."

"You kidding? He's crazy to leave his name."

"He didn't leave his name. He left the name of the man in the play. Mr. Tyrone. James Tyrone, Senior."

It was early dusk now. Donna sounded hoarse and lost. "Everything gets so fucked up sometimes."

We held hands for several blocks without talking. There was nothing to say.

13 ABOUT A MILE FROM REEVES'S PLACE, THERE was a Hardee's. We had some dinner. We sat in the car and the food smells filled the air. The sky was bruised. Skies like that always made me think of Good Friday. The air must have been similar, the black clouds low and roiling, the air chill and ominous.

We had our usual argument—for some reason I didn't want to defer—about Top Forty versus jazz and negotiated a settlement by turning the radio off altogether except for a newscast that said nothing new about Wade. Then we just sat back and watched teenagers haul their acne around in trucks with big wheels and cars with big mufflers. Finally, I put the car in gear and we went over to Reeves's.

"Excuse me," I said, "but I wonder if we could talk a minute?"

"You pushing *Watchtower*?"

"No, I'm not."

"Then what do you want?"

I showed her my American Security ID. I showed it to her fast, because any kind of scrutiny would show it to be the ringer it was.

She was eighteen and looked like a farm girl who'd moved to the big city. Her flannel shirt and OshKosh jeans said that about her. So did the pop country station in the background.

"We've been retained to do some further investigation into the murder the other night," I went on.

She looked at me as if she didn't know what I was talking about, and there was every possibility that she didn't. I started to explain further—seeing that I was getting no-where—when Donna stepped in.

"Hi," she said.

"Hi." The girl seemed a little surprised.

"We just need to ask you about the other night. Is that okay?"

The girl shrugged. She was pretty in a plain sort of way. "Sure. I guess."

"Were you home that night?"

"Yes. Studying. I work downtown during the day and at night I go to the community college."

"Did you hear anything?"

The girl shook her head. "No. The police asked me that already. I didn't hear anything at all."

"Did you see anybody?"

The girl grinned with embarrassment, as if she'd been stumped on a quiz show. "Not really, no. Just like I told the police."

"Did Michael Reeves get a lot of visitors?"

"I guess. I mean, I didn't pay all that much attention to him. He was actually kind of a snob. I mean, he gave you the impression that he was much better than you."

Donna smiled. "Yeah, I've known a lot of guys like that."

The girl beamed. Obviously she had a friend in Donna.

"How about earlier in the day? Did he have any visitors then?"

The girl started to automatically say no, but then she stopped. "I guess the police didn't ask me about that."

"Then you did see somebody?"

"Let me think. " She leaned her auburn head against the door frame. "I guess so. Yes, I did."

"What time was this?"

"Oh, between six and seven, I guess. I got home from work just before six because Dan Rather still had a few news stories to go, and then I took the first load of laundry down to the basement. That's when I saw the first one going into Michael's apartment." She shuddered. "God, when I called my folks and told them what happened, they wanted me to move out right away. But like I told them, if it's going to happen, it's going to happen. Right?"

"Right. Do you remember what this person at Michael's door looked like?"

"Oh, sure. His name was Lockhart. I'd seen him around before. He was one of the convicts. He told me that himself one day down in the laundry room."

"Lockhart hung around here?"

"Sometimes, sure."

"Did you hear Lockhart leave?"

"I saw him leave."

"When was this?"

"Oh, maybe a quarter to seven. *The Price Is Right* was on. Boy, that's really a dumb show."

Donna looked at me. I could see the smile playing on her lips. She wasn't going to lord all this over me. She wouldn't have to. I was going to lord it over myself.

"You said there was a second person," Donna said.

"Right."

"Did you know that person?"

"I saw her one other time. She came to Michael's and Michael made Lockhart leave for a while so Lockhart came down to my apartment."

"When was this?"

"Oh, a few weeks ago."

"Do you remember anything about the woman?"

"Just that she was very upset."

"How so?"

"Well, right in the doorway she slapped Michael's face. Real hard, too."

"This was a few weeks ago?"

"Yes."

"And she was here again the night of the murder?"

"Uh-huh."

"Did you get a look at her?"

"I'm not sure what you mean."

"Did she seem upset or anything?"

"Not . . . upset. I don't know how I'd describe it. Off in another world, kinda. Yeah. Off in another world."

I saw my chance and I was petty enough to take it. "Donna, why don't you ask her to describe the woman?"

We had a feminist rally going here. They both looked at me as if I'd just handed them a sack of doggie-do.

The girl scowled at me and then brought her attention back to Donna. "She was probably really beautiful when she was younger. Dark and very fine-featured with huge brown eyes."

I could tell from the way Donna's body gave a little shudder that she had recognized Michael's visitor, too.

"How long did she stay the other night?"

"I'm not sure, but I think she was up there quite a while."

"Did you see her come down?"

"Not really. But I heard her. She came down pretty fast."

"In a hurry?"

"Coulda been, yes." The girl looked at us. "I guess I should've told this to the police but they really only asked about later in the evening. You know, around the time when it happened. Then I didn't see anybody except the actor."

"Stephen Wade?"

"Yeah, him. Boy, I watched him on the tube all the time I was growing up. That's a really weird experience, identifying somebody like that to the police, I mean."

"That's all you can remember?"

She leaned her head against the door frame again. "I guess so. Sorry I haven't been more help."

"You've been a lot of help." Donna smiled. "Tell you what. We'll leave our card. If you think of anything else, you can call us, all right?"

"Sure."

"Why don't you give her a card, Dwyer?" Donna said sweetly.

"Gee, I'm glad I get to be a help," I said.

Donna took the card from me and handed it over to the girl. "I ran out of cards and need to get some printed," she said.

The girl looked at it. "God, you're really an investigator?"

"Yes," Donna said.

"I'll have to ask my counselor about that. About investigation, I mean. It's a field I should look into. I mean, you do really good at it."

"Thank you."

I nodded good night to the girl and she said to me,

"You're really lucky to have her for a boss. She seems really nice."

"Lucky isn't the word for it," I said.

Ten minutes later we stood in the back yard, in the shadows by the garage, in the gloom and rain, and Donna said, "So what's wrong with using the steps and just walking right in?"

"Gee, you'd think the boss would know better than that."

"I'm sorry if it hurt your ego, Dwyer, but it was probably very good for that girl to see. A positive role model and all."

"Well, once you get out of Detection 101, boss lady, you'll realize that we can't just walk right in there because that young girl will remember us just the way she remembered everybody else—and if the police ask her, they'll charge us with forcible entry. Among other things."

"So what're we going to do?"

"The fire excape."

"Are you kidding? We'll make too much noise."

"Not if we take our shoes off."

"Are you kidding?"

But I wasn't kidding, of course, so five minutes later we were climbing up the cold hard metal rungs of the ladder that stretched from the third floor to the ground. The rungs were so rusty that, with the rain, they felt as if they were covered with moss. By now we were hopelessly soaked, so the rain didn't bother us much, but the cold had gotten merciless. Donna had to stop a couple times to put one hand and then the other in her pockets. Gripping the hard edge of the cold rungs had numbed them. But then we went on, up into the black night. The third floor was completely dark, and we finally came to a window. It only took me a day or two to get the damn thing open. Once or twice I glanced behind me. It was obvious that Donna wanted to complain—she looked miserable, all wet and cold—but she didn't complain, nary a peep. So I was almost ready to forgive her her brilliance back there conducting the interview with the young girl.

Finally, I got the window open. I threw one leg over into the warm darkness on the other side, and then an arm, and then my head. Donna pushed up against my buttocks. "Are you stuck or what?"

The cold hard rain had taken its toll.

All we did for the first five minutes was stand inside next to a radiator and rub ourselves and hop up and down. We took off our socks, and Donna got us some towels. We dried our hair and then I took off my poplin jacket and wrung it out, and then Donna took off her sweater and blouse and kind of wrung those out. "That woman the girl was describing," she said. "It was Sylvia Ashton, wasn't it?"

"Yeah."

"If she was the last person to come up here, maybe she killed Reeves."

"That's what I was thinking. Especially with her background."

"What background?"

"Breakdown. I'll need to know more about it. We should check that tonight."

"I thought we were going to see Stephen Wade tonight."

"We are. We can check on Sylvia afterward."

"Dwyer, I hate to be a party pooper, but I'm afraid I'm going to need to sleep. Really."

"We'll get some sleep. Don't worry."

"Right."

I picked up my jacket from the floor. The playbill featuring David Ashton had fallen out. I pulled my jacket back on and stuffed the playbill back inside.

We searched for ten minutes before we turned anything up, and halfway through I would have bet against finding anything, because the police had probably taken everything that would have been of even remote interest.

But there it was, right on the desk, right in plain sight, so much so that the police must not have realized its significance.

"You find something?" Donna asked.

"I'll explain later."

"Boy, aren't we mysterious?"

If there'd been time I would have shown her the envelope I'd just picked up, the one with the peculiar but familiar logo on it, the one that explained a whole other side to Mrs. Bridges, and also where Lockhart probably fit into all this.

"I just want to wrap things up and get out of here."

"You're right, Dwyer. I just can't wait to get back outside in that cold and rain."

"Just keep looking."

But there was nothing else to be found, and a few minutes later we were heading down the fire escape.

"This has a very good effect on my cramps," Donna said.

"How's that?"

"I've got such a fucking headcold coming on, I hardly notice them."

I knew better than to laugh.

14 WHILE DONNA WAS TAKING A SHOWER, I SAT IN
her living room feeling a growing sense of
betrayal. I was getting the distinct impression
that old Mrs. Bridges had set me up. What I'd found in
Michael Reeves's apartment was an envelope bearing the
Bridges' personal logo, which meant that she and Reeves
had been in some kind of contact. That meant that she had
not told me the truth, probably about much of anything.

Donna came out with a towel wrapped around her head. I
tried hard not to notice her body in the green silk robe.
"Your turn," she said, sniffling. Then she bent over the
couch and looked at the envelope I'd set on the coffee table
to study. "What's that?"

I told her.

"So you think she lied to you?"

"I'm sure she did. This letter is addressed to Reeves, and
it's obviously written by a woman in her older years, and it's
her family logo."

"Why would she write Reeves?"

"I don't know. But after we meet Wade, I'm going to find out."

"You want some tea?"

"Sure."

She put the kettle on to boil and came back and gave me a hug. She smelled of perfumed soap and wet hair. She smelled wonderful. "I'll have the tea ready for you when you get out of the shower."

"Is that a hint?"

"No sense in both of us catching cold."

In the shower I kept wondering about Mrs. Bridges and why she'd write Michael Reeves, and I kept remembering Anne Stewart and her husband in the cabin. What had they been after? And why had Sylvia Ashton visited Michael Reeves the night of the murder? I put on some fresh clothes from the end of the closet Donna had allotted me and went back to the living room.

Donna hadn't put any clothes on yet. She sat in an armchair in front of the TV. MTV was on: Stevie Nicks working a little too hard at being ethereal. I should have kept my mind on Mrs. Bridges and Reeves and Anne Stewart and her husband and what Evelyn had been doing with Keech in her car, but I didn't. The thunder made me skitter across the floor like a scared animal. Donna must have been feeling the same way, because when I got there she put her arms out and drew me in. Our first few kisses were very tender—we were giving each other some inexplicable kind of reassurance—and then they were something other than tender. I pulled her up, and the way we stood we might have been dancing, she in her green silk robe, me in jeans and a T-shirt. I suppose we were dancing in a way, all the way over to the couch, where I eased her gently back. She said, "Wouldn't the bed be better?" but for some reason the couch had great appeal at that moment. Then all she said was, "I just put in a Tampax." I said, "I'll buy you another one," and she went off to the bathroom, where she spent what seemed like four or five hours. When she came back I turned out the light, and we made a slow sort of protective love with the rain and the violence unable to touch us as long as we were in each other's arms.

"I thought we were going to meet Wade," she said. This was half an hour later in my car. It was still pouring.

"We've still got an hour."

"So where're we going?"

"Over to the recreation center where Reeves held his acting classes for the ex-convicts."

"Why?"

"Well, first of all because that board at the halfway house said that Anne Stewart teaches tonight. Second, maybe some of the men there will know where Keech might be. I still want to know what he wanted in Reeves's office yesterday."

"Right. I forgot about that. I wonder what he was doing with Evelyn Ashton this afternoon, back at the cabin, I mean?"

"Exactly."

"Boy, this is starting to be fun again, Dwyer."

The Stanley Recreation Center shows the scars of being located in what passes for a ghetto in this city. It's a small brick building that used to be a school, but you wouldn't know it the way graffiti covers its walls and hundreds of yards of tape cover the cracks in its windows. Even in the rain there were teenagers out prowling, white and black alike, their eyes filled with fear and hunger. I read a book once about juvenile delinquency in the original thirteen colonies. I read it while I was in jail the weekend of my sixteenth birthday for going on a joyride in a stolen car. I wasn't driving but I knew it was stolen. Anyway, things changed after that weekend. The book taught me that there was nothing unique or special about being a punk, and forty-eight hours in the county lockup taught me that there were guys far more terrifying than I'd ever imagined and that I didn't want to be like them at all. That night, in the gloom and the downpour, I glimpsed kids as angry as I'd been and prayed they'd have the same kind of luck I'd had.

We parked next to a new tan Saab and got out. "Anne's car."

"Well, so far so good."

"Yeah, and remember that the next time you question what I do."

She goosed me hard enough that I gave out an unmanly yelp and jerked away from her. She's good at tickling, but she's twice as good at goosing.

The interior of the place changed our playful mood abruptly. The institutional green walls were lit by naked bulbs hanging from an exposed electric cable. Unused desks were piled along the walls, which were swollen with moisture. A tidy pile of petrified dog crap had been pushed off to the side of a door, and the graffiti alluded to virtually every part of the human anatomy. Down the corridor was a small gym where two young black men took turns taking devastating shots from past the free-throw line. Next to this was a smaller room where a group of elderly women listened to a public health nurse talk about Medicare benefits, or what was left of them now that the boys in Washington had decided to turn the country into an arsenal. A hand-lettered sign said ACTING CLASS and an arrow pointed upstairs. The deeper into the place we went the more it smelled like the schools of my memory—the aromas of floor wax and chalk dust, window panes cold with rain, steam heat, and the most ineffable smell of all, wood aging over the decades, a smell peculiar to old schools and old garages.

Just before we entered the classroom, I thought I heard a noise at the opposite end of the corridor in the deep shadow. I waited thirty seconds but heard nothing else, so I followed Donna up to the threshold.

There were half a dozen of them, all but one seated in ancient cane chairs. They were watching a tall guy in the center of the big empty room as he put his face in his hands, apparently trying to come into some sort of mystical contact with himself. He reminded me of a coke junkie on the downside. Over in a corner, near a barren steam-heat register, sat Anne Stewart and Keech watching the man in the center of the room. They seemed as fascinated as the ex-cons by whatever process was going on.

Abruptly, the tall guy threw his head back and screamed. For the first time I saw his face full on. His black hair needed cutting and his lantern jaw needed a shave, but what he seemed to need most right then was some kind of medical help to calm him down. His scream lingered in the damp, dusty air. It wasn't a theatrical scream, not at all. There was real frenzy and horror in it, as he proved by grabbing one of the empty cane chairs and smashing it against the register near where Anne and Keech stood. There was something orgiastic about the way he beat the chair into splinters. His dark eyes looked psychotic. Rheumy spittle shone on the edges of his mouth. He grunted in rhythm to his violence, and his grunts were far more obscene than any words he could utter. Donna put her face into my arm to hide her eyes. The poor bastard was coming undone. I looked around the room. In their way, the audience was just as spooky as the guy. They watched him with glazed fascination. They seemed to be in the same sort of psychosis that he was. One guy writhed in his chair. He appeared to be caught up in some kind of sexual rhythm. I glanced over at Anne and Keech. Their spell seemed broken now. Anne was putting out a hand to the crazy guy, muttering reassurances. Keech just looked scared. But the guy had found a new way to dazzle himself. He started pounding his fists against the register. He didn't seem to notice the blood that smeared his knuckles almost immediately or the bones that made cracking sounds like dry twigs snapping.

I crossed the room and got him under the shoulders and threw him into the wall, not hard enough to hurt him but hard enough to break his eerie concentration. A couple of the cons started to get up from their chairs and make menacing motions toward me, but they knew better—I had rage and animal fear on my side at the moment, and they sensed this and stayed where they were.

Not that the dark-haired guy was completely free of his frenzy. He took a good punch at me, a roundhouse right that he delivered with some expertise, and knocked me into the wall. The next one I saw coming and moved in time. I threw a block into him and slammed him back against the wall again.

Anne came up. "Karl, calm down, calm down! He's just trying to help you! All he wants to do is help you!"

At the last, Karl looked like Ahab. There was madness in his gaunt face and a crazed strength that scared me. I knew I wouldn't be able to withstand him for long.

Keech came up then. "Karl, were you taking the mescaline tonight?" In his yellow pullover sweater and designer jeans, Keech still looked the part of the perfect little man. But now he was frightened like the rest of us, and with Keech, fear spoiled the whole act. "Were you taking mescaline?" Keech was screeching.

One of the cons came up, a jittery man with bad teeth and a busted nose and brown eyes, like someone out of a Russian novel. "Keech, we was all takin' it. Shit, man, that's what Michael wanted us to do."

Anne said, "Byrnes, Keech and I told you last night that the class would be different from now on. We told you that." She sounded as if she were going to cry.

Byrnes shrugged. "It's like Michael always said, man, it's the one way to connect with the truth."

Anne nodded to Karl. "It seems to be an expensive price to pay." She looked at two other cons who'd come over. "Can you take Karl downstairs to the men's room and wash his face and see if that helps?"

They shrugged, mumbled. They were shabby, shambling men, and from the little I'd heard from Byrnes they sounded like jail house intellectuals, filled with half-baked ideas expressed with a hipness that was one part desperation and one part naïveté. Some of them would be basically decent men crippled by a mean and uncaring society; others would be (yes, there really is evil) mean and uncaring men who wanted to cripple society. I was beginning to sense Michael Reeves's kinship with this group—certain lawyers and social workers use cons in the same way. The cons have a great need to express their rage and self-pity and sense of doom, and people like Reeves show them how to do it—just as long as the cons show total allegiance. It's a cheap way to play God.

Karl was crying now, sobbing and writhing in the grasp of his friends. You could see a big stain where he'd peed his pants. His eyes were shot with red. He stank of sweat. He needed to throw up and sleep. Not much else would do him any good. When they took him away, he was still crying.

Donna drifted over. "Is he going to be all right? Shouldn't they take him to a hospital?"

Before I could explain, Keech said, "The hospital would call the cops and they'd bust him for parole violation. Using drugs is something parole officers frown on."

"Where did he get his mescaline?"

"Michael's desk," Anne said simply, as if it were perfectly logical that a desk would be used to dispense drugs. "In the next room he had a small office. That's where he kept it."

"Why mescaline?"

Keech shrugged. "He said it helped get at the truth."

"I thought this was an acting class."

Anne smiled ironically. "Michael always said that acting and truth were the same thing. You couldn't act well unless you understood the truth about yourself."

"So he fed these poor bastards mescaline," I said. "Great fucking guy."

"It just kind of got out of hand is all, Dwyer," Keech said. "I mean, for the first six months it was a great class. A very straight acting class. No drugs, anything. Hell, I got good enough in here to get the part at the Bridges Theater. The whole experience made being an ex-con tolerable. Then things changed, I guess."

"How?"

Anne said, "Michael started playing 'truth' games, the way acting coaches like to. You know, tell us something painful about your past. Well, as you can imagine, people who've been in trouble with the law feel a great deal of anxiety. Michael became more and more obsessed with getting to that."

Keech shook his head. "By the end, it was much more like some kind of group therapy than an acting class. Michael would just sit over there and watch us and never say a word. With the drugs, he didn't have to."

"You said 'us.' Did you take the drugs?"

He flushed. "Yeah. Yeah, I did."

"How about you, Anne?"

She stiffened. Despite her regal good looks, she seemed older now. "Yes." I thought of her and her husband in the cabin this afternoon. The ugly things he'd said to her. Their search for something unknown.

"Who else was in the class besides the men from the halfway house?"

Keech thought a moment. "Evelyn."

I watched Anne's face as Evelyn's name was mentioned. A tic appeared at the corner of her right eye. It was not difficult to guess that they'd both been rivals for Michael's attention.

"How about Lockhart?"

Now it was Keech's turn to look uneasy. "Lockhart?"

"Yeah. He's another guy from the halfway house."

Keech nodded. "Sure. He was a member of the group for a while."

"He was very tight with Michael," Anne said. "Very tight."

I studied Keech's eyes. "He's missing. You have any idea where he might be?"

"No, I don't."

We were having a stare-down. He won. I glanced back at the door, where some of the halfway house men had begun to file in. They looked sad and scared and I wanted to say something to them, but they'd already heard far too much from fellow cons who'd used them and dark saviors like Michael who'd exploited them.

"Why don't you do these guys a favor, Keech, and throw the fucking drugs away?"

"I'm going to. Believe me." He sounded young and lost.

For the first time I sensed something likeable in Keech. He was a polished little guy who came on like a hustler, but there was grief in him, and remorse, too. Anne must have sensed these things at the same moment, because she slid her arm across his shoulder. "It's going to be a different acting class from now on, believe me."

Keech said, "They haven't found Wade yet, I take it?"

I shook my head.

Keech's gaze got distant. "That's got to be a special hell."

"What's that?"

"Being stalked the way he is."

I nodded. Then I said, "There's a cabin out by the town of Brackett." Both of them visibly stiffened.

"You were both out there this afternoon. Keech with Evelyn, Anne with her husband. I think you know a lot more about Michael's death than you've let on."

Keech's face took on a look of misery that made him look like a very haggered boy. "Were you following us?"

"No. It was a coincidence." I waited. Neither of them said anything. "After visiting this acting class and hearing about how Michael conducted it, I'm starting to put certain things together. Probably not too long from now, I'm going to go to the police with what I know."

"You think one of us killed him?" Keech asked.

"I think it's at least a good possibility."

Anne said nothing. Just put her eyes to the floor and kept them there.

"Somehow, Lockhart figures in all this, doesn't he?" I waited for my words to unnerve Keech a little more. "Tell me about Lockhart, Keech."

"What about him?"

"How old is he?"

He shrugged. "Thirty, I guess. Why?"

"Is he bright?"

"Sort of, I suppose."

"What's he like to do?"

For the first time recognition shone in his eyes. He understood that I was going to force him to reveal something he probably didn't want to reveal.

"Just the usual stuff."

"What would that be?"

"Well, he always talked about girls a lot, so I guess it's safe to say that he liked girls."

"All right. What else?"

"And he always talked about baseball a lot, so I guess you could call him a baseball freak."

"Did you know him in prison?"

"Yeah, but not real well."

"What was your job in prison?"

"I worked in the prison library. I have a B.A., so they figured I'd be comfortable around books." He smiled at the irony of institutional wrongheadedness. "My B.A. was in physical education."

"What was Lockhart's job in prison?"

He did not look happy about telling me. "He worked in the infirmary."

"What did he do there?"

Again, the words seemed reluctant. "Oh, he was kind of a paramedic, I guess you'd say."

He was making me curious. Why wouldn't he want to tell me that Lockhart had been a paramedic?

"Was he good at it?"

"I guess so."

"What kind of things did he do in the infirmary?"

"Oh, he'd give you cold tablets and things like that."

"Anything else?"

"Shots. I guess."

"Shots?"

"Yeah, you know, injections." He glanced at Anne uncomfortably.

Anne said, "We give the men rides back to the halfway house and we're late already. Do you mind?"

So my conversation was ending. "Sure," I said. I'd learned something, but I wasn't sure what.

Anne turned to the men. "If you'll go downstairs and get in my car, I'll be right down."

When they were gone, she said, "Dwyer, I'd like to speak to you alone, if that's all right."

"Of course."

I smiled at Donna. Keech seemed agitated about the whole prospect. He gulped very loudly.

We went over to the corner by the register that Karl had tried to demolish. She said, "Wade killed him."

"I'm not sure of that."

"I love Stephen. I really do. But he killed him. Stephen's a drunk with a violent temper, and he knew that getting fired from a job out here would ruin what was left of his reputation."

"Anne, what are you trying to tell me?"

She looked as if she were trying very hard not to cry. "There's no point in digging around in all this. Wade killed him. He really did."

"What were you and your husband doing at the cabin this afternoon?"

Now the tears came. "It has nothing to do with Michael's death. Nothing."

"I'm not so sure of that."

Keech called out. "We've got to go, Anne!" The agitation was still obvious in his voice.

Anne said, "Please, please, Dwyer. Please just leave things alone." Then she was gone, over to Keech and down the stairs and into the rainy night.

For a long time Donna and I stood just holding each other, saying nothing. Finally, she whispered, "There's something down at the end of the corridor."

"What?"

"Sssh. Not so loud." She leaned closer again. "There's somebody down by the end of the corridor."

Now I whispered, too. "How do you know?"

"I heard something sneak up the corridor and then sneak back.

"Shit," I said.

"What?"

"I wish I had my gun."

Her grip stiffened on me. "God, I didn't even think of that."

"What?"

"Maybe he has a gun."

"Well," I whispered.

"Well, what?"

"Well, I guess there's only one way to find out."

15

HE WAS DOWN THERE, ALL RIGHT.

At first, as I moved into the hall, it was almost like being blind. Moisture from the night and my nerves stuck my shirt to my back. In my hand I carried a piece of plumbing pipe I'd found in a storage closet. I'd made Donna stay behind.

He moved.

From what I could gather, as my eyes began to adjust, he was behind several big packing crates. The noise was his jacket scraping against the rough boards of the crates. A rasping, like rats in walls.

I knew he might be any sort of vandal or vagrant, but I didn't think he was. There were plenty of hiding places on the first floor. He had chosen to be near the classroom because the acting class interested him. I was beginning to form an impression of who he might be.

The pipe in my hand was rusting from my sweat as I saw him dart across the hall from one big crate to another.

"Stop!" I yelled. Maybe he'd think I was a cop. But you

couldn't say I impressed him much. The mildewed air was silent except for my breathing. No sign of anybody ambling out with his hands up. He wasn't going to make it easy. For either of us.

Toward the opposite end of the hall, in the muzzy light spilling from the classroom, I saw Donna peek out. Exactly what I told her not to do, in case the guy had a weapon and fired at me.

I turned back toward the packing crates, and that's when he jumped me.

He came at me in an awkward tackle, getting me around the waist and putting me hard up against the wall. The pipe dropped from my hand, clattering in the darkness on the floor. Just before he kicked me in the side of the face, I heard Donna start screaming. He got me one more time in the face and took off. Now I yelled, warning Donna, and tried to get to my feet.

What happened next, there in the spill of light from the classroom doorway, was not without a comic aspect. Donna stuck one of her long legs out, sort of like a confused chorus girl who didn't quite know the dance routine, and the man was obliging enough to stumble over it. He wore a shabby overcoat, which made the windmilling motions of his arms look even more cartoonish. By the time he reached the floor, sprawling and sliding, he had sworn so many times it was quite impressive. That was when she jumped on him, the way you jump on a trampoline, with your bottom leading and your arms outstretched. "Hurry, Dwyer! I don't know what to do next!" she said on the way down.

When she landed, he started groaning and scrambling to his feet. He tried to punch her, but he had no leverage and missed. In return she gave him a dainty little slap. The next one she gave him was not dainty at all.

I got him by the shoulders of his coat and dragged him

into the classroom. I was still scared and mad enough that I wanted to pay him back for the kick in the face, so I got a good sharp fast one off to his ribs.

"God," Donna said, coming into the room, "who is he?"

"I have a feeling we've just met Lockhart."

"Fuck yourself," the man said.

"Boy, so far," Donna said, "he seems like a delightful person."

Probably not even Lockhart's mother loved his face. He had feral brown eyes and a feral pink mouth and feral pointed ears. He needed a shave and a shower. Donna was right. He was delightful.

"I think you can help us," I said.

"I think you're full of shit."

"That may be. But I still think you can help us." My face hurt but I'd be damned if I'd give him the satisfaction of rubbing it. "Who killed Reeves?"

He smiled. "Your buddy. Wade."

"No, he didn't."

"Gee, then I must've been listening to the wrong station. Seems like every time I turn on the radio or the TV, they're talking about how many cops are out looking for him." He winced. Looking down at him, the way his eyes narrowed with pain, I wondered if I should have kicked him quite so hard. I probably could have made my point with a bit less violence.

"Why were you out in the hall?"

He looked at Donna. "I was taking a piss."

She smiled at him. "Gosh, I'm really offended and shocked. Taking a pee in a school corridor."

"I don't want to kick you again," I said.

He grimaced. "You try it, motherfucker, and see what happens."

I stepped on his hand, quickly enough that he didn't even try to get it out of the way. I stepped down hard.

"God, Dwyer, c'mon." It was Donna talking. "God, look at him." She looked down at his hand as if she were going to be sick.

"Why were you out in the hallway?"

"Fuck yourself."

I stepped down harder. "Tell me."

He screamed.

"God, Dwyer, please," she said.

"Donna, for Christ's sake, I've got to know why he was out there."

"But you're hurting him."

"Look at the left side of my face."

She looked. "God, what happened?"

"This guy you're so worried about kicked me."

"Why, you bastard," she said to him.

"So will you please go somewhere if you can't take it?"

"Why did you kick him in the face?" she said to Lockhart. He was too busy grimacing to answer.

"Step on his hand," she said. "He deserves it." Then she said, "But not real hard, you know, Dwyer? Not *real* hard."

"Donna."

She made a face. I eased up a little, out of deference to the woman I love, and that's when he grabbed my ankle and knocked me over, and Donna right after me.

He ran to the door to the stairs. We were maybe a half-minute behind. His feet clattered on the staircase. Below, he careened into two old ladies coming from their Medicare class. They screamed. He kept on running.

I nearly ran into the same two ladies myself, trying to get to him. His flight had been slowed just enough that when he reached the front door I could grab the sleeve of his raggedy overcoat. It ripped away from the rest of his coat. He whirled around, slamming into the doorframe, and then he got his composure again and started into the downpour.

I saw it happen from the doorway.

The street was narrow and the pimpmobile was going at least twenty over the speed limit. It was long and pink, and even with the windows rolled up you could hear the disco music from the tape deck. When it hit Lockhart, it didn't slow down a bit, nor did it slow down when it reached the corner. If anything, it went faster, and then it disappeared.

Donna was two steps behind me. We started out into the rain. We didn't run. We knew he was beyond help. She slipped her hand in mine. "God, Dwyer, I don't know if I'm up to looking at him. Do you mind?"

"Uh-huh. You go back in the school where it's dry."

"I don't give a damn about the rain now, Dwyer. I mean, after what happened to him." She just stood there with her arms folded, huddling into herself.

I nodded, understanding, and set off for the street. Another car had come along. In its headlights I could see Lockhart clearly. He reminded me of a dead dog in the road. You want to look away but something terrible in you—something that recognizes your own eventual death—holds your eyes there. I thought of how I'd stepped on his hand, the pain I'd given him, and the wild sad look of him then. I felt like shit. I bent and took his pulse. I looked up into the broad face of a sixtyish black man in a plastic raincoat and shook my head. Behind him more headlights appeared. I was surprised to see that it was the pink pimpmobile. A swarthy white man got out. He wore a tatty gray three-piece suit, a very white shirt, and a very red tie. He had a business card held out. The black man looked at me and shrugged. Which one of us was supposed to take the card, and why?

"I didn't see him, mon," the swarthy man said in a

Jamaican accent. "I did'na see him." He was so bombed the black man had to help him back to his car.

I found Lockhart's wallet in his coat and put it in my pocket. I went back to Donna and said, "We need to get out of here. Fast."

On the way to the car, she said, "God, look at your hands." I held them out in the dim streetlight. They were covered with Lockhart's blood.

THE HUGE CHURCH LOOKED LIKE A FORTRESS put up against the night itself. Lightning cracked the sky as we ran up the broad stone steps through the brutal and relentless rain.

Inside there were huge shadows thrown by the votive candles of blue and green and yellow and red, and incense that smelled holy and exotic at the same time. Statues of the inscrutable Virgin and the weary Joseph looked down on us as we moved up the wide center aisle, past the empty pews and the stations of the cross carved in stone. Where Jesus crumpled beneath the cross He carried, Donna shook her head and said, "I really should start going to mass again, Dwyer."

At the east side of the long communion rail, a squat man in a dark coat knelt, head bowed. Donna and I looked at each other. Wade? I went up close enough to get a look. The man, curious as I was, glanced up at me. He had a pugged Irish face whose shape was lost somewhat in bulldog jowls. He appeared to be a spry seventy. "Are you Mr. Dwyer?'

115

I nodded. For the first time I realized that he was wearing a priest's collar.

"Then you'll be wanting the sacristy," he said in the middle of my old neighborhood.

Donna came up next to me.

He looked at us both and smiled briefly. "It's all right. He's waiting for you." He indicated the sacristy with a thick hand. "But you, Mr. Dwyer, would you mind returning to speak to me?"

"Not at all, Father."

"Good, then. Go. He needs to see you. Badly, I'm afraid."

"Thank you, Father."

"Yes," Donna, sounding young, said, "thank you, Father." We went up the steps leading to the altar. "What a neat old priest," Donna whispered. "I really do have to start going to mass again, Dwyer. Really. Will you go with me?"

"Sure," I said.

She squeezed my hand.

The sacristy, which was where priests prepared themselves for mass, was in more deep candle shadows when we reached it. I looked in. The long, wide room smelled of communion wine and rain from an open widow at the opposite end. It smelled of cold air, too. We went in and found a man sitting in a big chair, which probably belonged to the monsignor. He had black hair and a beard and wore a flowered shirt and a double-breasted sport jacket, both of which were at least ten years out of date. In the candle gloom, his white plastic shoes were a dirty joke. A pint of whiskey lay at a casual angle in his left hand.

Donna gripped my arm. She wasn't sure and I wasn't sure either, and it was damned eerie, looking at him and not being sure.

"Stephen?" I said.

He said, "Thanks for coming. Christ almighty, I really appreciate it."

"Oh, Stephen," Donna said and went to him. She hugged him tight. He hugged her back. In the light I could see that as he hugged her he clung tight and kept his eyes closed.

When they parted, Donna came back to stand by me. I said, "You need food or anything?"

He shook his head. "Father Ryan took care of me. Isn't he a sweet old bastard?"

"He sure is," I said.

"Gosh, Stephen, you shouldn't call him a bastard," Donna said.

He laughed. "I guess you're right, kid. Strike 'bastard.' Let's say he's a sweet old guy."

"There," she laughed back, "that's much better."

"This was my parish when I was a boy. He gave me my first communion."

"They're looking for you everywhere," I said.

"Don't I know it. A couple of times on the street, I figured they came pretty close to nabbing me. One traffic cop took a long, hard look at me, let me tell you."

"I've got to be honest, Stephen."

"What's that?"

"I'm a little surprised you're still on the sauce."

"It's my only comfort, m'boy."

"Bullshit."

"Dwyer," Donna said. "C'mon. Gosh. He's our friend."

I didn't know why I was angry, exactly, but I was. I reached out and waggled my fingers at the bottle. He started to hand me the bottle and then took it back. He killed what was left in a single, noisy, vulgar gulp. Then he handed me the bottle.

"Cute," I said.

"Don't go sanctimonius on me, Dwyer. It doesn't become you, believe me."

Donna stepped between us. "God, you two, come on."

I took a deep breath. "I'm sorry, Stephen."

He stood up and came over to me and we kind of half-embraced and slapped each other several times on the back.

"You all right?" I said.

"Pretty fucked up, actually." He looked up at the ceiling. "It feels kind of weird to swear in a place like this."

"Yeah."

"I saw a newscast tonight. I don't think the cops are even considering anybody else for the murder."

"I'm afraid that's true."

He looked at me. He didn't look like Stephen Wade at all. "I didn't kill him."

"I know."

"God, Dwyer, thanks for saying that. I mean, after I slept off the drunk, I reconstructed the night. I really didn't kill him."

"Yeah," I said. "Now all we've got to do is prove it."

He laughed. He didn't sound happy. "So are you developing any leads?"

"Maybe too many." I described our day—our visit to the halfway house where Lockhart was missing, the cabin where we saw Evelyn Ashton and Keech and then Anne Stewart and her husband and where we found the old playbills, and the letterhead from Mrs. Bridges in Reeves's apartment.

His first response was, "Oh, yeah, the cabin. That's quite a place."

"You've been out there?"

"Sure. Many times. If Donna wasn't here I'd tell you about all the women I took out there."

"I'll plug my ears," she said.

"When did all this happen?" I asked.

He leaned back against a counter where crystal wine cruets shone like silver in the slow, silent flashes of lightning. "The old days. Back when David Ashton and Sylvia Bridges and I were sort of like the Three Musketeers."

"Back in your twenties?"

"Very early twenties. Hell, Dwyer, you forget that I was on Broadway when I was twenty-four." Even in these circumstances, he couldn't quite let go of his ego. Maybe that was why I liked him so much. He was a bit of an asshole, but he pulled it off with great style. Most of us don't pull it off at all.

"Did you know a Dr. Kern?"

"Ah, yes. The great doctor. Actually, we tried to cast him as a bad guy, but on balance he was probably pretty decent. He took great care of Sylvia during all her problems."

"What problems?"

"Well, as I think you know, she was diagnosed as schizophrenic very early on. You know how her mother is— I think she always blamed Sylvia herself for not having a strong enough constitution to overcome her problems. Mrs. Bridges isn't one of my favorite people.

"Anyway, when Sylvia and her mother had the falling out over David, Dr. Kern stepped in and really took control of Sylvia's life. He asked Mrs. Bridges for permission to keep Sylvia out at the cabin, and asked that the entire Bridges family stay away. This went on for three or four months, I guess, and finally Sylvia came around. She'd been hanging right on the edge, believe me. Right on the edge." He looked at his empty hand. He obviously wished that there were something liquid in it.

"You mentioned a falling out over David. What was that all about?"

He snorted. "Mrs. Bridges always wanted Sylvia to fall in love with me. You know, Sylvia's a very good actress, and when she was involved in a play, she managed to keep her head screwed on relatively straight. So Mrs. Bridges encouraged her to be in plays and to spend time with me, because, frankly, I was always a much better actor than David. He was better looking, but the poor guy just never had much talent, I'm afraid."

"But Sylvia fell in love with David?"

He nodded. "More than fell in love with him—she almost adopted him. Almost. David had a terrible background. Grew up with a drunken uncle, was on the streets when he was fourteen. There was always a waif side to him, and a sad side, too. I suppose that's what Sylvia loved about him so much. She saw some of herself in him. Things might have been different for them if they hadn't had to get married."

"That's what set Mrs. Bridges off?"

"Yes. She's an arch-conservative, and this was back in the early sixties. She saw it all as nothing more than a way for David to wile his way into the family riches."

"He seems to have done very well for the theater."

"Of course he has. He's made it into a first-rate regional theater. But you'll never catch the old bitch admitting it."

"So you don't think he got her pregnant on purpose?"

"What if he did? He's been a good husband, believe me. He took damn good care of her after the affair at the cabin that night."

"What affair?"

"One of Kern's assistants—she didn't like him. You know how you just inexplicably don't care for some people? Well, it was like that with her and this fellow. And one night, when David was on one of his road tours, she got very incensed with the assistant and stabbed him."

"Stabbed him?" The image of Michael Reeves came immediately to mind. So did Sylvia's mysterious visit to him on the night of his death.

"Uh-huh."

"Did he die?"

"No. She just grazed him in the arm. The family paid him a great deal of money. No charges were ever pressed. I should have stopped it, but I was out in the living room—" He paused. "I was getting drunk."

"You were there that night?"

"It was a weekend. They have several guest rooms. Sometimes when David was on the road, Dr. Kern would call and ask me if I'd stay over. He always said it was good for her spirits. So I'd come out. Hell, man, I cared a great deal for Sylvia and, face it, I didn't mind spending my time in surroundings as posh as those. My old man worked in a foundry, pal. That was the lap of luxury."

I took the playbills from my coat and handed them to him. He took them over to the candelabra and held them up to the light. A smile brightened his face. Even with his disguise you could suddenly see that he was Stephen Wade. He looked much younger.

The first playbill he waved at me showed the three of them together. "We were really brats back then. Even Sylvia. Really filled with ourselves. Did you ever see the Truffaut film *Jules and Jim*? You know, the two men who love the same woman? We saw that and took it deadly seriously. We were inseparable after it—the film gave us permission, I guess." He shook his head. "Then David started going on the road." He held up the other playbill. "It sure didn't do Sylvia any good. Hell, it didn't do him any good, either."

"Where did he go on the road?"

He shrugged. "Oh, those were the days when packaged

tours were still big, when a fading movie star could get lots of money to put a musical together and play the smaller markets. They were a real grind, and I never knew anybody who really got anywhere doing them. But David wanted to be a successful actor more desperately than anybody I've ever known. So he'd go on these long tours and Sylvia would come apart. I'll give him one thing, though. He changed after Evelyn was born. He's been a hell of a good father to her. He gave up his acting ambitions and has been a damn good husband and a damn good father." He handed me back the playbills. "That's a lot of years ago." There was awe in his voice. Contemplating time does that to us.

"I need you to think about something. Hard."

"What?"

"Sylvia."

"What about her?"

"Can you remember her ever getting violent again?"

He stared at me through the flickering shadows. "God, are you trying to say you think Sylvia stabbed Reeves?"

"It's a possibility. A neighbor saw her there the night of the killing."

"Saw Sylvia?"

"Yes."

"God." He went over and sat down again in the chair. He put his head in his hands and then he broke. He didn't cry exactly. It would have been better if he had. "It's all so goddamn crazy, Dwyer. I'm scared and confused and—" He paused. "Dwyer, there's some communion wine over there. It's still in the bottle so it hasn't been blessed. I need some, Dwyer. I'm not kidding you. I'm getting hot and cold flashes and my stomach's going to shit. I'll beg you if you want me to, Dwyer. I'll goddamn beg you, I promise."

"Dwyer," Donna said softly.

"Where is it?" I said.

"In that top cupboard."

I went and got it and brought it back. It was a quart of grape wine made by monks in Vermont.

He stared shaking then, just as he reached for it, and then he did start crying. I unscrewed the cap for him.

He drank. For a long minute he didn't seem to be aware of either of us.

"I'm going to see the priest," I said to Donna.

She nodded and went over and knelt by Wade and started gently stroking his sleeve.

The priest was still at the communion rail, praying. In the red and green and yellow votive lights he looked like a Christmas-card priest. He crossed himself and stood up. "You're his friend. You know what we should do," he said.

"I know."

"He's in sad and sorry shape. He shouldn't be running."

"Is there a phone I could use, Father?"

He led me out of the church and across an open stone courtyard to the rectory. The rain hit us cold and hard for maybe thirty seconds. It made a lot of noise in the metal drainspouts. My feet got soaked in the puddles. The rectory smelled of a roast-beef dinner from earlier in the night. I used a phone by a hall closet filled with yellow dust mops scented with sweet polish. I called Edelman and told him what was going on. I must have said ten times at least, "Just be easy with him, Edelman. Just be easy with him." When I was finished I turned back to the priest and said, "Now I know how Judas felt."

"Now don't be getting melodramatic the way he always does, Dwyer. It's a curse we Irish suffer from. You may be saving his life and none of this has a damn thing to do with Judas Iscariot, if you'll pardon my French."

I laughed. Wade was right: he was a sweet old guy. We went back out into the rain and the puddles and the tinny sound of the drainspouts.

In the sacristy, Wade was still in his chair and Donna was

still kneeling next to him. I went into the shadowy light and stood in front of him and said, "I have to tell you something."

He opened his eyes and looked up. "I know what you're going to say."

"You can believe it or not, but I did it for your sake."

"I know. I can't run anymore, anyway, Dwyer. I'm too goddamned tired." He saw the priest behind me. "Sorry, Father."

Donna said, "Is there anybody you want us to call, Stephen?"

This time he did break and he broke all the way. "That's the irony," he said, crying. "Every friend I've got in the world is right here in this room."

Edelman did it the way I asked him. Two cars came, one with Edelman, the other with two uniformed officers.

Edelman came into the sacristy, doffing his hat when he saw the priest. He nodded to me and Donna and then went over and stood beside Wade.

"They're not going to hurt you, Mr. Wade," he said, nodding to the two uniformed cops who stood nearby in yellow slickers, dripping water. The overhead lights were on now. Everything looked too real and harsh. Wade took off his beard. Theatrical glue stuck to his face like a skin rash. He looked silly and sad. He looked up at the priest and said, "Would you give me a rosary, Father?"

The priest reached in his pocket and handed Wade a circle of black beads. "I'll be praying for you, Stephen."

For the first time Wade, his eyes red from tears, laughed. He looked at the two uniformed cops and said, "Good, Father, because I've got a feeling I'm going to need it."

Edelman nodded to me. Then they took Stephen Wade away.

17

As we pulled up in front of the Bridges Theater, Donna said, "Isn't it kind of late?"

"I guess right now I don't much give a damn."

Between us on the seat lay Lockhart's wallet. It was a cheap brown cardboard thing. Some of his blood was on the fold.

She covered my hand with hers. "It wasn't your fault, Dwyer. C'mon, now."

"I should open the damn thing and look inside. But—" I looked down at it. "I can't touch it. It's like having some sort of phobia."

"You want me to do it?"

"I shouldn't have stepped on his hand so hard."

She didn't say anything.

"I shouldn't have, should I?"

She sighed. In a tiny voice, she said, "No, I guess you shouldn't have."

Then I couldn't say anything.

"I wish you hadn't asked me that, Dwyer, because I love you so damn much, but I don't want to lie, either."

"I know."

"But it wasn't your fault he died. I mean, you didn't push him out into the street."

"Yeah."

"Here, I'll open it." She picked up the wallet. She got blood on her hands right away. She looked at me. Then she took Kleenex from a box in the glove compartment and said, "It wasn't your fault, Dwyer. Do you understand?"

She opened the billfold and thumbed through everything. She found a ten and four singles. A picture of Lockhart and a plump girl in a bikini on a summer beach. A Milwaukee Brewers baseball schedule. A Trojan. She held the rubber up to the light and said, "God, that's really classy."

"I've got one in my wallet."

"Bull."

"I do."

"I know better because I looked through your wallet."

"You did, really?"

"Yeah, one day I needed money. I guess I should have told you. Does that make you mad?"

"Uh-huh."

"Really."

"No."

"You sure?"

"Positive. Because if I got mad at you then you'd get mad at me."

"For what?"

"Because one day when you were on the phone talking to Chad I got kind of pissed or jealous, I'm not sure which, and I started going through your purse."

"God, Dwyer," she said.

"Hey, you can hardly afford to get sanctimonious."

"A wallet's one thing but a purse is something else."

"You are stone fucking crazy, you know that?"

"No, really, Dwyer. There's only so much you can find in a wallet, but a purse can be filled with all sorts of things. I mean, there's a mathematical difference. Looking in a purse is a lot worse than looking in a wallet."

"Right. So what else is in there?"

She put the Trojan back. The next thing she found was a business card. "Trueblood Medical Supplies," she read.

She handed it over. I thought of Lockhart being an orderly in the prison infirmary and stuck the card in my pocket.

She leaned over and kissed me. "At least you're feeling better. Even if you did look in my purse."

"You're really pissed about that?"

"Not *real* really, if you know what I mean."

"You're deranged."

I opened the door and got out. My clothes were wet enough that the constant rain didn't matter any more. Donna got out, too. In front of us the marquee was dark, hundreds of dead little bulbs battered by rain. The six front doors leading into the theater were also dark, like the doors on a movie set shut down for the night.

We went around to the side and found Stan. He was sweeping up by the dressing rooms. He nodded hello. "You just can't seem to stay away from here, can you?" He smiled, rubbing one hand on his gray janitor's uniform.

"Actually, we'd like to see the Ashtons, if that's possible."

"Well, I'll call up and see what David says," he said.

"I'd appreciate it."

While he went over to the elevator, I walked from the nearest wing toward the stage. My footsteps were loud and hollow. I peeked out into the empty theater. Donna came up behind me. "God, if I ever got on a stage, I'd freeze."

I kissed her. It was like high school. Furtive. And very sweet.

Stan came over. "David said for you to come on up."

He'd caught us kissing. Donna was blushing.

"We just heard on the news about Wade," David Ashton said as we stepped off the elevator. He wore a blue polo sweater and tan slacks. With his blond hair and Scott Fitzgerald features, he looked like an aging tennis pro.

I listened for excitement in his voice, but there wasn't any. He was just reporting the facts. He led us into a living room that in my neighborhood would have passed as a ballroom. Sylvia was sitting in front of a huge TV screen. In red lounging pajamas, her dark hair tousled, she seemed young and quite desirable. Only the dark glasses spoiled the effect. Instead of seeming mysterious, they smacked of neurosis, the tic of a perpetual mental patient.

"Sylvia, Dwyer and his lady friend are here."

Sylvia raised her head from the screen. She acknowledged our presence by rattling a glassful of ice in our direction. David dispatched himself instantly. He took her glass, went to a dry bar, and with almost chilling medical precision made a drink: three parts this, two parts that. Then he brought it back to her and put it in her hand.

He came back to us and said, "Sylvia's taking some of her heavier medication. It won't hurt her to have it with alcohol, but it makes her very drowsy." How convenient, I thought, in case the police ever wanted to question her about anything.

"It's odd that you should show up now," David said. He led us past an almost funereal dining room with a long shining table and a low-hanging chandelier toward the front of the penthouse where he and Sylvia and Evelyn lived.

"Why's that?"

"About ten minutes ago, Mrs. Bridges asked if I could help locate you."

I sighed. "Was this right after you learned that Wade had been taken into custody?"

"Yes. Why?"

"Oh, nothing. I suppose I'd better go see her."

He gave me an ironic smile. "I'd appreciate it, Dwyer. I don't like to disappoint the old woman."

I smiled back. "And I thought *I* had some lousy jobs."

"It's not that bad usually. She only gets upset with me when I clearly fail to live up to the 'Bridges standard,' as she puts it."

I kissed Donna on the cheek and followed Ashton down the hall. At the doorway leading into Mrs. Bridges's part of the penthouse, the servant took over again.

"I should warn you," he said on the way to her room. His shoes squeaked.

"I don't think you have to."

"You have upset her."

"So has the rest of the world."

He laughed. "At least you have a sense of humor."

"I'm assuming that I get a blindfold and a cigarette."

"Mrs. Bridges doesn't approve of smoking."

He knocked once on her door and then stepped back. Far back. He was no fool.

She was still a kewpie doll. Tonight she wore a powder-blue nightie. She had painted her nails. She was still surrounded by photos of the famous from the first half of the century and by the flowers that covered the odor of her illness. Her blue eyes blazed so intensely they were almost comic. "Young man, you have let me and this theater down very, very seriously."

I couldn't help it. She—or her money or the room or her age or her illness or all those things put together—

intimidated me. I said, "I," but that's all I said. I didn't seem to have another word to put with it. She took advantage of my mealymouth by applying her own words to the silence.

"I wanted you to save the reputation of this theater and you didn't."

"No, I haven't," I said, finding my voice. "Not yet."

"And what's that supposed to mean?"

"Wade didn't kill Reeves."

"You sound awfully certain of that."

"I am."

"And you have evidence of it?"

"No, but I have a lot of facts that point in a lot of different directions other than Wade."

"Such as?"

"Such as Michael Reeves was probably blackmailing somebody."

"Who?"

"Maybe several people."

"I don't want your damn games. I asked you a direct question. Who?"

I let her have it, and with no small degree of relish. "You, for one."

"Me? You're suggesting that Michael Reeves was blackmailing me?"

I took the envelope from my pocket, the one with her personal logo on it. "I found this in his apartment."

She snatched it from me and looked it over. "You're a liar."

I shook my head. "You said you didn't want any games, Mrs. Bridges. I'm not playing any. I found that envelope in Michael Reeves's apartment. You must have sent it to him."

Her cute little face was fiercer than ever now. "And I'm saying to you that you're a liar."

"There's only one other way that it could have gotten there."

"And how would that be?"

"Sylvia took it there the night of the murder."

I'd gotten the impression that Mrs. Bridges was very good at keeping her face from revealing secrets, but a big, cumbersome secret struggled across her features then. She looked guilty as a little girl with her fingers in Mommy's jewelry box.

"So you know," I said.

"Know what? You're playing games again."

"No games, and you know damn well what I'm talking about."

"Don't speak to me in that tone," she said.

"Then don't try to waste my time."

"Exactly what is it, Mr. Dwyer, that you're accusing me of?"

"I'm not sure yet."

"Well, that's a very impressive piece of detective work."

"All I know for sure is that your daughter went to Michael Reeves's apartment the night he was murdered. Now I'm beginning to believe that she brought him an envelope from you that contained money. That would lead me to suspect that you, directly or indirectly, were paying blackmail to Michael Reeves. And that's exactly what I'm going to tell the police when I leave here, Mrs. Bridges. They'll want to talk to Sylvia."

She reached over and pressed a button. David Ashton's voice came on the intercom. "Yes?"

"David, I want you to give Sylvia that new prescription from Dr. Kern. I want you to give it to her immediately."

"Is something wrong?"

"Don't ask me any of your damn foolish questions. Just give it to her."

"All right, if that's what you want."

She looked triumphant. "Sylvia won't be interviewed by anybody for quite some time, Mr. Dwyer. As a matter of fact, before the night's out I strongly suspect that she'll be in Dr. Kern's clinic. And Dr. Kern can be very persuasive."

"Is that how he kept her from going to prison when she stabbed one of his workers?"

"How did you know about that?"

"You wanted me to look into the case, remember? When you start looking into things, you learn secrets sometimes."

"I want you to leave."

"What was Reeves blackmailing you with?"

"Did you hear what I said? I want you to leave."

"There's an innocent man in jail tonight."

"I'm beginning to wonder if he is innocent. He sounds more and more guilty to me."

"You'd ruin the theater's reputation to save Sylvia, wouldn't you?"

The anger faded. She looked old. "Do you have children?"

"One. A boy."

"Wouldn't you do nearly anything to save him?"

"Of course."

"Then don't be foolish. Of course I'd save Sylvia before I would the theater."

I was suffocating in the flowers. "He was blackmailing you, wasn't he?"

The hand she flung at me scarcely had any strength. "Just leave, Mr. Dwyer, leave now."

On our way back to Donna, the servant said, "I've never seen her so exhausted like this. You must have disturbed her a great deal." He was smiling as he said it. When we reached the other half of the penthouse, Donna explained that David Ashton had had to excuse himself. I knew what that meant. He was busy putting his wife into a form of brain death so that nobody, especially the police, could ask her any questions.

In the car, Donna said, "Dwyer, we've got to get some rest. Think of all we've been through in the last twenty-four hours."

"I'll drop you off."

"Dwyer, you too, all right?"

"I feel fine."

"You look like shit."

"Thanks."

"We're not that young anymore."

"I'm thinking of Stephen," I said.

She was silent. Then she said, "I'm being selfish."

"So I'm not dropping you off?"

"Right," she said, sounding weary. "You're not dropping me off."

18

TRUEBLOOD MEDICAL SUPPLIES WAS HOUSED IN a small brick building a few hundred yards from a railroad siding. In the rain and fog, the green and red railyard lights were bright as beacons. A lone switch engine lurched by. As we walked toward the building, the engineer tugged twice on the air horn.

A light shone through a grimy window. I peered in past the metal mesh. A naked overhead bulb lit long, tall rows of supplies on deep wooden shelves. The place appeared clean and orderly and prosperous. I rattled the door knob. I hadn't really expected it to be open. "Let's try the front," I said.

We walked around the corner to where a big glass window read TRUEBLOOD MEDICAL SUPPLIES. From there I could see a small, tidy front office with three gray metal desks from the sixties, a fake red flower in a slender glass vase on each. I tried the front door. Zip. Zero. Nada.

"You still haven't told me—" she started to say.

"—what we're doing here exactly," I finished for her.

"Exactly, smart-ass."

"Well, in prison Lockhart worked in the infirmary. Out of the prison he lived at a halfway house, where he had nothing whatsoever to do with medicine. But he had a card from a medical supply house in his wallet."

"Boy, that is weird."

"Now all we have to do is raise somebody and ask him a few questions."

"There isn't anybody in there."

"There should be."

"At this time of night?"

I nodded toward the back. We stood under an overhang. In the moonlight the rain drops looked fat and silver. "You didn't notice the little decal on the door back there?" I said.

"What little decal?"

"It's from the Thornton Security Agency. A bull's-eye."

"Uh-huh. I didn't notice it."

"Well, that supposedly means that Thornton keeps a man on the premises every night."

"So there's somebody in there?"

"Yeah, and apparently he's asleep because I sure rattled the hell out of the back door."

Without missing a beat, she said, "Are you hungry?"

"God, I wish you hadn't said that."

"Meaning you are."

"Yeah. Sort of."

"You know what I'm thinking about?"

"Before you tell me what you're thinking about, I'll tell you what I'm thinking about. I'm thinking about my waistline and about how my agent gets on my ass every time he sees me these days. Donna, I've really got to cool it with the food."

"Yeah, I guess that's sensible."

We stood under the overhang some more and watched the fat silver raindrops and our chilled silver breath.

"So why don't you tell me what you were thinking about?" I said.

"It'd probably be better if I didn't."

"Hell, there ain't any calories in mental pictures."

"I was thinking about Denny's." Junk food is her specialty.

"Yeah, what about Denny's?"

"Well, you know that breakfast they serve, with a cheese omelet and hash browns on the side with one of those little containers of Kraft's grape jelly?"

"Yeah."

"That's what I was thinking about. My relatives down South always serve food like that. You're going down there in June with me, right?"

"Right." I liked the South, and I'd heard so much about her relatives that I wanted to meet them. But right now I wanted to go to Denny's and have the food she'd just described.

I was just about to take her hand and lead her around back, whether to the door again or to Denny's I wasn't sure, when the door behind us opened and a chunky woman with a butch haircut and a big Magnum said, "This ain't no place for hanky-panky. This is private property."

"Bertha," I said.

She squinted at us with steely blue eyes. In her blue Thornton Security uniform she could easily have been a guy, and when I'd worked with her there had been occasional speculation that she actually was, or had been before the miracle of surgery. She was wide and squat and a good woman in a gruff way.

"Dwyer?"

"Yeah."

"Dwyer, you dipshit, what're you doing out here?"

"Trying to get inside."

"You'd think a former cop would know that B and E is against the law." With a quick practiced glance, she assessed the tall and casually beautiful Donna Harris. "How did you ever talk her into spending time with you?"

"I'm still wondering myself."

She tilted her head toward the inside. "You up for some coffee?"

"Sounds great," Donna said.

Apparently I now had an official spokesperson.

Bertha Lamb led us down a corridor to a tiny lunchroom with a formica table and a microwave that didn't look big enough to hold a donut. On top of the cabin-style refrigerator sat a Mr. Coffee with a full pot. Bertha poured coffee into "personalized" mugs and handed us each one. I drank from Mona's cup, hoping Mona didn't have gum disease or something. Bertha raised her cup with a heavy competent hand, almost in a toast, and said, "Were you the asshole who was rattling the back door?"

"Yeah, why?"

"Well, I've had a spell of stomach trouble, so I was incapacitated for a while." She nodded to a door that showed the brush strokes of a bad green paint job. The sign read LADIES. "Puts you in a hell of a bind, let me tell you. You can't move but some fool is rattling anyway." She smiled at Donna. "What do you see in this hot dog, anyway?"

"Not much, now that you mention it," Donna said sweetly.

"Now I want you to tell me about this place," I said.

"Trueblood?"

I nodded.

"Started working here last week. The plumbing's bad, their subscription to *Time* ran out a couple months back so they've just got old issues, they've got a Scanray security

137

system that isn't worth diddly-squat, and one of the secretaries keeps a jumbo package of Switzer's licorice on her desk. Unfortunately, Thornton makes us take a polygraph test every month, so if I so much as took a bite of the stuff, I'd be out of a job."

"You think the place is strictly legal?"

"Huh?"

"I mean, have you noticed anything funny going on? Late-night deliveries, anything like that?"

"You on a case?"

"Sort of."

"I wish Thornton would let me moonlight like that. Hell, I get tired of being a baby-sitter for alarm systems. I wish I could work on an actual case."

"So have you noticed anything?"

"Uh-huh."

"Damn."

"Sorry, Dwyer."

Donna said, "Do you know anything about the owners?"

I looked over at her, impressed. I should have thought of that myself.

"You a detective, too?"

"No, I'm an editor."

"An editor?"

"Yes, of an advertising magazine."

"Oh, I see." But obviously she didn't. She put a fat finger to her sulky lower lip. "The owners. Hmmm. Nope. I don't remember anything except for a plaque in one of the offices. Shows a bunch of guys a long time ago cutting the ribbon to open this place up. That mayor—Dandridge—was in the picture, the one who went to prison? He was the one cutting the ribbon."

"Mind if we go see the photo?"

She shrugged. "Hell, no. Come on."

We followed her. As we walked, I asked her about Lockhart: she didn't know anything about him. She moved like a rowboat in rough water. Her thighs were so short her Magnum almost touched her knees. We went back to the front office. All of us looked at the desk with the big black slab of Switzer's licorice on it. "You'd think the bitch would at least have decency enough to keep it in her desk," Bertha said.

We went through a dark door. Bertha flipped on the lights. A mahogany desk the size of a ping-pong table lay before us. It was covered with photos of a blond middle-American family. All the kids would grow up to be George Bush. There were two miniature flags on the desk, one U.S.A., one state. The rest of the desk was so bare it looked like a prop. Bertha pointed to a faded photograph behind the desk, reverently framed in silver. "There."

We went over and looked at the six men. Each wore a suit of the sort that Edmund O'Brien wore in *D.O.A.* (one of my favorite actors in one of my favorite movies). At the right edge of the photo you could see a black 1948 Buick, fat and formidable. I scanned the men, their faces. At the fourth one I stopped.

"God," Donna said. "Look." She was ahead of me.

"Somebody you know or something?" Bertha asked.

I grabbed Donna's hand. "Maybe," I said, and started to turn toward the door.

"Hey, Dwyer, you going to clam up on me, you bastard?"

"Bertha, look, if I told you what was going on, you'd be liable to tell Thornton all about it, right?"

She shrugged unhappily, knowing I was right. "I guess. Yeah."

"So I'm going to do you a favor and not tell you anything at all."

"Gee, thanks, Dwyer." She looked and sounded as if she was going to cry. I felt bad. I liked her.

"But we'll have you over to dinner once we get all this resolved," Donna said.

Bertha brightened. "Say, you're one hell of a nice lady, you know that?"

"Nice to see you, Bertha," I said. And we were gone.

"It was him, I know it was him," I said.

"In the photograph, you mean?"

"Yeah."

"You mean Dr. Kern?"

"Yeah. He had a mustache and a lot more hair and he had on that strange double-breasted suit, but it was him."

"You're right, Dwyer," Donna said. "It was definitely him."

"But what's he got to do with Trueblood Medical Supplies?"

"Right. And why did Lockhart have the medical supply's card in his pocket?"

"I'm not sure."

"You sure you're not sure?"

"What's that supposed to mean?"

"I mean, maybe you know or think you know but are keeping it to yourself."

"No. One thing they teach you on the force is to form as few opinions in advance as possible."

She didn't say anything for a time. Just watched the windshield, the way headlights and then muddy water splashed across it.

"You really don't have any ideas, Dwyer?"

"Not yet. Sorry."

"Damn." Then she curled up, foetuslike, next to the door.

The sanitarium was on a hill. It was brick, big and friendly even in the gloom. It might have been the campus of a small liberal arts college. Definitely not the sort of place that mad scientists hung out. Our headlights swept the right wing; on the third floor the windows were barred. For a moment that struck me as ominous, but I thought it through. Some mental illnesses inspired violence. Barred windows, in such cases, made sense. To the right of the front door in front of neatly trimmed hedges was a white sign with gold embossing that said HAVENHILL. We pulled up in front of it and got out. Next to us was another car that looked familiar. "Boy," Donna said, "this really is starting to come together."

"Yes," I said, "maybe it is."

The car was a silver XKE. It belonged to Evelyn Ashton's father. It was the same one we'd seen her and Keech in.

We went up to the double doors and knocked, safe from the rain beneath a wide porch roof. There were enough lights on for the Cubs to play at night.

The girl who opened the door was nineteen at most, but she was one of those fair earnest blondes who at that age are already on their way to being matrons. She wore jeans and a turtleneck sweater underneath a blue smock. I hadn't seen eyeglasses like hers since the fifties. An English teacher I hadn't liked much owned a pair just like them. The woman's favorite novel had been *Giants in the Earth*, the only novel I know that makes *Silas Marner* read like Judith Krantz.

"Yes?" the girl with the glasses said. She sounded only a bit nervous about visitors coming this late.

"We'd like to speak with Dr. Kern."

"I'm afraid he's busy right now," she said. A smidgen of chocolate malt in the right hand tuck of her stern but erotic mouth spoiled her seriousness somewhat.

"It's very important," Donna said. "It could be life and death."

"Oh," the girl said. Surprisingly, she didn't move or even say anything—just that little neutral "Oh." She stood before us, chocolate smidgen and all, thinking it over. "Then I suppose I'd better get him, hadn't I?"

"If you would, please," Donna said.

"Come in then."

While the girl went down a white hall long enough to approximate a near-death experience, we stood dripping in the vestibule. Donna took my hand. Her skin was hard from the cold. She looked around, then shoved it in my pocket. "Sorry. It's the only way I can get my hand warm." When she finished with the left, she inserted the right. At least she was careful about the exact placement of her hand. She didn't lead me on.

Dr. Kern wore an English hunting jacket and an open white shirt. His mussed hair spoiled the effect of casual control he wanted his clothes to give. So did his frenzied glance. He looked as if he'd just finished helping deliver triplets.

"I really don't have time to see you," he said, obviously annoyed at our presence.

The girl smiled, pleased that he disliked us as much as she did.

I took the TRUEBLOOD MEDICAL SUPPLY business card from my pocket and showed it to him. "We found this tonight on the body of an ex-convict named Lockhart. I believe you know him."

All he said was, "Marsha, why don't you go back to making your rounds?"

"Really, Doctor?" She was tremendously disappointed.

"Really, Marsha."

She went back down the white tunnel. Maybe at the end of it she'd find beings more to her liking than we'd been.

Kern said, "I was going to call you—or somebody."

"Me?"

He glanced around, as if somebody might be eavesdropping. "My life has started to come unraveled and I don't have any control over it at all."

"If you wanted to talk to me, why did you look so aggravated when you saw us a minute ago?"

He ran a shaky hand through his hair, then waved the hand toward another part of the sanitarium. "Evelyn and her friend Keech are here. They've been telling me things—" He shook his head. "I'm afraid I'm not reacting well to pressure tonight. When I saw you, I thought maybe you were here to help Evelyn. I'm not thinking clearly."

"Help Evelyn. What does that mean?"

"She's accused me of trying to talk her mother into confessing."

"To what?"

He brushed a hand on his jacket and said, "Why don't we go into the small study? Evelyn and Keech are in the larger one down the hall."

"All right."

We followed him. In the study were a fireplace and enough books to start a small-town library. He poured us brandy from a cut-glass decanter. For some reason, my first taste of it made me sneeze. Donna made a production out of pantomiming a big "God bless you." She considered it terrible luck to miss a "God bless you" in these circumstances.

When he was seated in a leather chair, Dr. Kern said, "Evelyn thinks I want her mother to go to the police and confess."

"Confess to what?"

"To Michael Reeves's murder."

"Do you think she's guilty?"

He studied his brandy, then raised his head. "I think it's a possibility."

"So do we," Donna said. She explained how Reeves's neighbor had told us about seeing Sylvia Ashton there not long before the murder.

"My God," Kern said.

I leaned forward in my chair. "Now I want to know about your relationship with Lockhart."

He smiled unhappily. "Until Evelyn brought him up half an hour ago, I didn't even know I had such a relationship. I thought she'd just come out here because it's her birthday today. She usually drives out. I'm her godfather. But Lockhart—I'd never heard of him till today."

"I don't follow you."

He got up and poured himself more brandy. We declined his offer of another round. He sat down and said, "In high school, Evelyn worked at the medical supply house I own half of."

"Trueblood."

"Yes."

"I'm surprised a girl as wealthy as Evelyn would work there."

"That was David's point. He's always been of two minds about the money he married into. On the one hand he likes it, on the other he feels that it inspires many false values. He wanted his daughter to know 'the real world,' as he always calls it. So he asked if she could work at the medical supply house, and of course I said yes. She was a very good worker. She came back three different summers during her college years. All the employees liked her a great deal. That's why it was so easy for her and Lockhart to find somebody to help her."

"With what?"

He studied his brandy. "What I'm going to tell you may prejudice your thinking. It puts Evelyn in a bad light, I'm afraid."

"There's a man in jail tonight who's in terrible shape, Doctor. Right now, he's who I'm thinking about."

He finished his brandy. "I assume by now you know about the 'truth' games Michael Reeves liked to play?"

"Yes."

"They were very characteristic of a certain kind of psychosis, the sort you find in many powerful people in our society. Presidents who want the FBI to spy on private citizens, corporate heads who sic detectives on their employees so they can know what their people do in off hours, members of Congress who are always pushing for loyalty tests of various kinds. Michael Reeves was a lot like that—but he went further."

"How so?"

"Were you aware that some of the ex-convicts in his acting class used mescaline?"

"Yes."

"Well, he went even further than that. He convinced Evelyn to help him obtain sodium pentothol—what people call 'truth serum'—which is one of the things Trueblood happens to stock. Because Evelyn knew everybody there, she didn't have any trouble finding an employee who needed money and bribing him into giving her pentothol. This went on for some time. Evelyn got scared, so Lockhart started paying the man off himself, getting the pentothol, and bringing it back to his good friend Reeves."

"Where does Keech fit into all this?"

"Keech, for all his crusty surface, even for all his psychotic tendencies, is actually in search of a reasonable life. He's been in love with Evelyn for quite some time. Of

145

course, he had to pretend otherwise in order to save his ego—he knew of her affair with Reeves. But yesterday he went to her and told her how he feels."

I thought of what the director of the halfway house had said about Keech. Keech's supposed affection for Evelyn could be a clever ploy to cover up his own complicity in the murder. "Do you believe him?"

"I guess so. Why?"

"I'm just considering all the possibilities."

"Well, when I tell you about the sodium pentothol, you'll see even more possibilities," he said.

"Reeves used it on his acting class?"

"Yes. At first, anyway. When they were under the influence of the mescaline and supposedly pushing toward the 'truth' he wanted them to find, it was no problem for Lockhart to inject them with it."

"He'd been an orderly in the prison infirmary."

"Exactly."

I was beginning to see the inevitable direction of what he was saying. "But he didn't stop with his acting class, did he?"

"No. Eventually he got around to everybody—Keech, Evelyn, even Sylvia Ashton."

"Sylvia?"

"My God," Donna said.

Dr. Kern's face flushed. "The bastard. If I had known what he was doing to her, I might have killed him myself. Her grip on reality is tentative enough as it is—but to play with sodium pentothol—" I believed his threat. He seemed young and strong suddenly. "Under the influence of the drug, he had no difficulty finding things out about people. Evelyn and Keech, both of whom were very much in his grasp at the time, took the drug willingly, as part of their 'search for truth,' as part of learning all about 'real acting.' You can ask Reverend Jim Jones about how all that works.''

"How about Sylvia Ashton?"

He shook his head. "She didn't take it willingly. She took it because she knew that Reeves had started to blackmail Evelyn."

"How did you know that?"

He looked surprised that I didn't know. "Why, Evelyn herself told me. After she realized what sort of person Reeves was, and what he was doing to her, she came to me in a real panic."

Now Lockhart's position in all this was coming clear, too. As Reeves's closest cohort, Lockhart knew that Reeves had very profitable blackmail material stashed someplace. That's why Lockhart had asked Stan if he could look in Reeves's office, and why Lockhart had come to the acting class the night of his death—to search for the blackmail material.

"What about Keech? Why was he with Evelyn the other day?"

"I encouraged Evelyn to see him. Keech is in love with her, much as neither of them are willing to admit it. At this point in her life, that's a very good thing." He frowned. "Plus, they have one other thing in common—Reeves was blackmailing Keech, too."

"What did he have on Evelyn?"

He cleared his throat. "Evelyn told Reeves all about a hit-and-run accident she'd had as a teenager—this was under the influence of the sodium pentothol, of course. The man she hit wasn't killed, but he was injured badly. It's just the sort of story Evelyn's grandmother would pay a lot of money to keep out of the papers. Reeves knew she'd be willing to pay." He shrugged. "As for Keech, he revealed that he'd been involved with a seventeen-year-old girl shortly after getting out of prison. Technically, that's not against the law in this state, but it could help an unsympathetic parole officer send you back to prison. So he had to start paying Reeves whatever he could, too."

"God, Reeves was really into power," Donna said.

"Reeves knew Sylvia pretty well—knew that she was weak," Kerns said. "He may even have seduced her. There are times when Sylvia feels very lonely—sometimes even when she's surrounded by people she loves—and then she's very vulnerable to seduction. Much more so than most women."

"You're making a very strong case against her," I said.

He nodded glumly. "I know."

"If I was a police detective, I would call her in for questioning—at the very least. Especially if I knew about the incident with the knife when she was in her early twenties."

"You really *have* been looking into this."

I watched his face. "Do you think she killed him?"

"I'll repeat what I said before."

"Which is what?"

"That I think it's a possibility."

"There's at least one other possibility."

"What's that?"

"The way David Ashton has been so careful to cover for his wife."

"You think David Ashton did it?"

"That's another possibility. But I think there's an even better one," I told him.

"You've lost me."

"What if he knew that it was his daughter and not his wife who killed Reeves? By being so protective of his wife, he makes her appear all the guiltier. He might be thinking

148

that Sylvia could get off with an insanity plea. But Evelyn—well, she's mentally sound, and she is his daughter."

Something tightened his eyes, and he looked for a moment as if he were going to tell me something terrible. But all he said was, "As you say, there are a lot of possibilities."

I studied him. Something I'd said had troubled him. But what? He stood up. "I'm afraid I've got to get back to Evelyn. She needs calming down."

Donna frowned at me. She must have noticed Dr. Kern's sudden strange attitude, too.

He held out a hand and we shook. He contrived a smile. "Now I know why people pay to see psychiatrists. Just by talking this through, I feel better." But he sure didn't look better or sound better.

Marsha appeared as if by magic and showed us to the door. She hadn't wiped the chocolate smidgen off her mouth. I'd expected more from a girl like her.

19 "WHAT A WAY TO SPEND YOUR BIRTHDAY," Donna said an hour later.

"What?" I'd alternated my time between reading the sports page (the Cubs had lost again) and looking at the playbills we'd taken from the cabin, the one featuring Stephen Wade, Sylvia Bridges Ashton, and David Ashton, the other featuring Ashton alone.

We were sitting in Denny's. We'd just finished the breakfast of eggs and hash browns that Donna liked so much. There was a drunk guy sitting at the counter. I was going to feel a little safer when he got back on the road.

"I was just thinking of Evelyn," Donna said. "Today is her birthday. I mean, given everything that's going on, what a lousy birthday."

"Yeah."

"You look like you're trying to levitate those playbills," she said.

I smiled. "Yeah."

"Why do you keep staring at them?"

"I suppose because I'm trying to learn something."

"What?"

"I don't know."

She raised one eyebrow—she knows how to do such things. "You wouldn't be holding out on me, would you, Dwyer?"

"I wish I was."

"You look sort of cute, with your hair all frizzy from the rain, I mean."

"Thanks."

"Hold that thought. I'll be right back." She leaned across to whisper to me. "I'm down to my last Tampax. We'll have to stop at a Seven-Eleven."

"Hell, we'll just go to your place."

"If we do, we'll be tempted to sleep, and I can tell from the way you're acting that you don't want to sleep."

"No, I guess I don't."

"What're we going to do, then?"

"See what Evelyn is up to now."

"Seriously?"

"Seriously."

Evelyn's car wasn't in back of the theater, so we drove over by the halfway house. Traffic was thinning. The rain had become a fine mist. Evelyn's car was parked in front of the halfway house, and Evelyn and Keech were sitting in it. We went down the street and parked at the far end where we could see Evelyn but she wouldn't notice us.

"He was a spooky guy, when you think of it," Donna said as we sat there.

"Who?"

"Michael Reeves."

"Yeah, he was."

"He even got to Sylvia Ashton. You would think he would have been scared of pushing her over the edge."

"He thought he was on to something."

"Like what?"

"I'm not sure. But I don't think he would have toyed with Sylvia unless he thought he could get something very specific and useful from her."

For a time we said nothing. We sat and watched the black trees shine with rain.

There was a moment of light as Keech opened the car door and got out. He waved good-bye to Evelyn and went inside the halfway house. Evelyn pulled away. I waited half a minute and went after her.

"You have any idea where she's going?"

"No," I said.

"Good," Donna said, "it's more fun that way."

Five minutes later Evelyn pulled up next to a car phone stand. She dropped in her coins, waited for a response, and then began to talk in very animated style. At one point she made a fist and banged the side of her car. Then she calmed down and kept on talking; something seemed to have been resolved. We sat half a block away, in the parking lot of a closed Hardee's, watching. Then she hung up and pulled away, and we went after her.

She led us through the downtown section, along the river where the most interesting part of the city, the old brick buildings of the original settlement, had given way to tall office buildings that stood half-empty thanks to poor planning.

At first I had no idea where she was going, but then she started hanging sharp lefts and sharp rights, and gradually I realized that she was taking a circuitous route back to the theater.

The place was dark and looked almost as if it had been

shuttered permanently. Rain made the surface of the parking lot gleam. Evelyn pulled around the corner of the rear entrance and sat there. That surprised me—I had expected her to park and go upstairs. She lived here.

"Maybe she's going someplace else," Donna said.

I shrugged. "Hell, I don't know what's going on."

We sat there five more minutes. The jazz station was doing a mini-Brubeck concert. I hadn't heard Brubeck in years. It was like rediscovering Marc Chagall.

A figure in a dark coat ran from the shadows of the theater to Evelyn's car and got in very quickly. Then we were off again.

"Who was it?"

"I'm not sure," I said.

Ten minutes later I knew where we were going. The city street gave way to a two-lane highway. All I could see were brown cornfields flashing in the glare of my headlights.

Evelyn and her passenger were headed for the country, and probably to the cabin where we'd been the day before.

THE WIND WAS WHIPPING THE TREES TO THE
breaking point. Large branches had been
ripped out and hurled onto the pavement
leading to the cabin road. Half a mile before the entrance to
the road I'd cut the headlights so that Evelyn would think
the car behind her had turned off.

"Boy," Donna said, "this is really eerie." And it was.
The wind was rocking the car and the branches snapped like
bones beneath our wheels. The radio was off so I could
concentrate better. For light there was just the green glow of
the dash instruments. Donna sat on the edge of her seat,
harnessed in her safety belt and gripping the dashboard. In
my police days I used to have a partner who rode just like
that when we ran the siren.

"We're going to have to walk from here," I said.

"Are you serious?"

"Of course."

We were down the cabin road, but not close to the house.
We couldn't afford to get close—they'd see us for sure.

"Boy," Donna said. But she got out anyway.

The walk took ten minutes. We got so wet so fast we didn't care anymore. Donna sneezed once and said, "God, I hope I don't get a cold and have my period at the same time."

Believe me, I devoutly wished the same thing. Colds made her crabby all by themselves. With her period in the bargain . . .

Once she stumbled off the road. "Ick," she said, pulling her foot from oozing mud. But beyond that she didn't say anything else. She just got back on the road and trooped right along next to me. She did favor her muddy foot a bit. Like an injury.

We came up on the west side of the cabin. Downstairs, the windows were yellow rectangles in the murk. We climbed up next to one of the windows and looked inside.

The woman in the dark coat stood in the middle of the living room as if she were lost. Her coat dripped rain. Her eyes stared fixedly at something I couldn't make out. She made no effort to remove her coat.

"Sylvia," Donna whispered. "Why would Evelyn bring her out here?"

I shook my head. I had an idea but I didn't want to say.

A minute later Evelyn appeared in the middle of the living room. She took her mother's coat, hung it up in a closet, and led her mother over to a divan next to the fireplace. Sylvia sat down, moving mechanically, like a zombie. I thought of the drugs David Ashton had given her earlier.

"Boy," Donna said, "this just gets weirder and weirder."

Evelyn disappeared again.

We stood silently in the whipping wind and soaking rain.

The air smelled of damp wood and fetid vegetation from last winter.

This time when Evelyn reappeared she bore a tea kettle and two delicate little cups. She poured hot tea and handed one cup gently to her mother.

"I wonder if she'd sell us some," Donna whispered.

After Evelyn got a fire going, her blonde hair glowing beautifully in the flames from the crumpled newspaper, she went back to the divan and sat down right next to her mother. They said nothing. They just stared straight ahead into the fire. They might have been strangers seated next to each other on a bus.

Finally, Evelyn spoke.

"Damn," I said. I pushed myself as close as I could to the window. I even pushed my ear against the cold pane of glass. But I couldn't hear her. All I could do was watch.

At first Evelyn carried on a one-sided conversation. She spoke emotionally, setting her teacup down and using her hands to gesticulate dramatically, but Sylvia just sat there without responding. She wore a prim white blouse and designer jeans. Her tousled black hair gave her the aspect of a mad and aging princess. If she heard her blonde daughter, she gave no sign.

Then Evelyn slapped her. A single sharp slap. Her mother's head jerked back. She spilled her tea on her lap. She put her hands to her face and began sobbing. Evelyn stood over her. She was shrieking. For the first time, I could hear her. "Mother, you have to remember what happened that night. They're going to blame you for Michael's murder!"

But I could see that her mother scarcely understood Evelyn's words and probably didn't even know where she was.

Then the violent moment subsided. Evelyn went over and

knelt at her beautiful mother's knees. She put her head against Sylvia's legs. Absently, Sylvia began to stroke her daughter's hair.

"Actually, that would make a really sweet photograph," Donna whispered. "It'd make a nice birthday present. They seem to be a family that really needs to be together. Remember what Stephen told us about how David used to be on the road and how it upset Sylvia so much?"

"Yeah," I said.

"Chad used to do that to me."

We were standing out in a bitter night and she was going to make it even more bitter by talking about her ex-husband. "I sorta did the same thing, too. He had this friend named Jay. We used to go out to dinner a lot when Chad was out of town. Until Jay made a pass at me. I never told Chad, though. He would have killed both of us."

"Why would he kill you if Jay was the one who made the pass?"

"That's just the way Chad is."

One more reason to like Chad.

And then I thought of something—or at least I started to think of something. There was a date on the playbill about David Ashton's road tour. I thought of the date, and then about Evelyn's birthday being today, and about how long Stephen said David's road trips used to be—

And then I didn't think of anything at all. Because all I had time to do, in response to the sound of snapping in the undergrowth behind me, was turn and see the stock of a Browning hunting rifle come smashing into my face.

Donna screamed, or at least I think she did, and that was all I remembered.

21

IN MY COP DAYS I WAS KNOCKED OUT ONLY once. I was in a union bar trying to break up a fight and somebody hit me from behind with a bumper-pool cue. I felt two sensations at once, the shutdown feeling of slipping into unconsciousness, and a terrible arctic cold spreading from my face to the rest of my body. When I came to, I was in an emergency room on a gurney, and I had the impression that my father had visited me. When the intern came up, I said, "Is my dad here?" and he said "I don't think so, sir." Then my wife stepped up and said, apparently in a play for pity on my behalf, "His father is dead." The intern nodded as sagely as he could, as sagely as any twenty-five-year-old snot can.

When I came to I saw Donna bent over me, her red hair draping her face like a cowl. "Boy, Dwyer, thank God, really, thank God," she said. "I mean, for you being alive and everything."

Then I felt the goo, right where my hairline had started to recede. At first it felt like paste but of course it was blood and of course it was mine. We were in an attic surrounded by many ancient cardboard boxes and a couple of trunks.

"Would you do me a favor?"

"Sure, Dwyer, what?"

"Put your hand in my back pocket."

"God, Dwyer, are you joking at a time like this?"

"Right, Donna, my fucking head feels like somebody dropped a cement block on it and I'm telling fucking jokes."

"Well, God, you don't have to get so mad. I mean, you've got to admit it's kind of a weird request and all. I mean, right after you regain consciousness."

"Are you going to do it or not?" I was getting angrier by the moment.

Beneath her breath, she said, "Boy, what an asshole." Then I threw my weight to the left, lifting my left cheek off the floor, and she squeezed her hand down my pocket and said, "Okay, now I've got my hand in your pocket. What should I do next?"

"Is there a handkerchief there?"

"Yeah."

"Then take it out."

"All right. I've got your handkerchief out."

"Good. Now hand it to me."

"Delighted."

She gave me the handkerchief and I applied it to where the rifle had connected. Then I started the long and painful process of standing up.

I had just gotten my right palm flat on the floor for leverage when she said, "He's going to come up here and kill us, Dwyer. That's what he said. David Ashton, I mean."

"Where are we?"

"He made me help carry you up to the attic. There's a

stairway down, but he's got the door locked at the bottom and there's only the one window, the weird little round one up there.''

"Wonderful.''

"What?''

"I said wonderful.''

"Oh.'' She was on her knees next to me. She got her arms under my arms in a kind of hammerlock, and I'll be damned if it didn't help me get to my feet without much trouble.

I spent two minutes leaning againt a dusty wall. I wanted to make sure the dizziness was going to subside at least a bit before I tried walking.

"Boy, Dwyer, you knew it was Ashton all along, didn't you?''

I just looked at her. "You're hyperventilating.''

"How can you tell?''

"Some bastard's down there with a hunting rifle and he's going to come up here and kill us and you're just jabbering away.''

"Well, at least you didn't attribute it to my period.''

"Seriously, will you shut up for a minute and let me think?''

"I can't help it, Dwyer, I'm scared, and when I'm scared I talk my ass off. I used to drive Chad crazy sometimes.''

"Gosh, that's hard to believe.''

"All right,'' she said, making a silly little gesture with her fingers and mouth, "it's locked.''

Rain pounded the roof. On the little window it sounded like BBs. I could hear nothing from below. I held out my hand. "How about holding on to me?''

"Where are we going?''

"Down the stairs.''

"But the door's locked.''

"You forget all the keys I've got."

"Hey, yeah."

" 'Hey, yeah.' Take my arm, okay?"

She took my arm. My head hurt and I really needed to pee, and I felt feverish from the pain. The steps seemed twenty feet apart. We moved slowly. I could smell sweat from my own pits, or maybe it was from Donna's pits. We'd spent a long day alternating activity with anxiety, so probably neither of us were up for a fancy dinner party.

At the bottom of the stairs was a door framed by yellow light from the other side. The door was locked.

"What're we going to do?" Donna whispered.

That was when the gunshot came from downstairs.

"Use one of my basic Boy Scout tools," I said.

I knelt down and got out my pocket knife and proceeded to have at the door. The house still echoed with the gunshot. My head still hurt from all the abuse of the past day. Donna knelt next to me, looking cute and lost and scared and wet.

"You going to pick it?"

"I'm going to try."

"I thought you did it with credit cards."

"Some locks you do with credit cards."

"But this isn't one of them?"

"Right."

"It's a good thing you were a cop."

"Please."

"What?"

"Ssshh."

"Oh, yeah. Right."

So I started. Various second-story men I'd busted during my days on the force would have paid a great deal of money to see this. A great deal.

I started sweating, and my headache got worse. I turned the knife right, I turned the knife left, I wiggled, I waggled, I waffled. The mother still wouldn't open.

161

Then Donna said, "Maybe you're not doing it hard enough."

"Donna, believe it or not, I know what I'm doing." I could hear the pissiness in my voice. Pissiness is not my best quality. I tried a patient explanation, but it probably just came out patronizing. "I mean, this isn't a matter of brute force, it's a matter of delicacy. Of finding the tumbler and turning it."

"God, Dwyer, just jam the darn thing in once. What've we got to lose?"

So I jammed the darn thing in once, and of course the darn thing (which is to say, the motherfucker) opened right up.

We knelt there looking at the next room as the door swung open.

"Now what?" Donna said.

"Now we sneak down the hall and see what's going on."

"I'm scared."

"So am I."

"Yeah, but you're better at pretending than I am."

I put out my hand. She felt it twitch.

"Boy, Dwyer, you really are scared."

We left the room on tiptoes and went down a long, dark hall to the top of the stairs. We huddled in the gloom and listened. There was just the rain. I could smell gunpowder.

"What're we going to do?" she breathed into her cupped hand against my ear.

"Go downstairs."

She pantomimed. "Are you crazy?"

I led the way down. With each step I pictured the layout of the large first level. The open living room. The fireplace. The dining room in the left wing. The kitchen in the right. There had been a screened-in back porch, too.

I was almost giddy when we reached the bottom. Fright

does that to you sometimes. Blood was running into my eyes.

The living area was well lit and empty. The smell of gunpowder was especially strong there.

"Did he take them somewhere?"

I shrugged. She took my hand. We went into the dining room. We found Sylvia Ashton in the corner.

At first, remembering the gunshot, I thought she was dead. But in the shadows I saw her mad, lovely eyes glint, and as I moved closer, even above the rain, I could hear the soft rhythm of her breathing. Donna knelt on one side of her, I knelt on the other.

"Where did he take her, Sylvia?"

She said nothing.

"She isn't his daughter, is she, Sylvia? She's Stephen Wade's daughter, isn't she?"

Nothing.

"That's what you told Michael Reeves when he used sodium pentothol on you, wasn't it? That's why David killed him, isn't it?"

Donna and I looked at each other across Sylvia's tousled dark hair.

"David knew that your mother would push him out of the family if she ever knew that Evelyn wasn't his child. That's why David had to protect your secret—he'd be penniless, otherwise."

She raised her head. "He's been a good father to her. Better than Stephen ever would have been."

Then she began sobbing. She fell into Donna's arms, an eternal child seeking eternal succor.

I went out through the house to the screened-in back porch. I could smell rain and fresh earth and chill night. I had no idea what I was going to do.

"Please, Dwyer, don't come any further."

The voice jarred me. Not because it was so menacing, but because it wasn't menacing at all. It belonged not to David Ashton but to Evelyn.

He sat in a white porch swing, huddled into the corner of it, and he was a mess. He'd been shot in the stomach. He was crying and trying to vomit.

She sat across from him, on a metal coaster that squeaked.

She looked up at me. "He grabbed the gun and tried to shoot himself. I tried to knock it out of the way. He got shot in the stomach."

She was in shock. It was then that I noticed the shotgun sitting next to her.

Just then he moaned and you could see on the floor where some of his innards had dropped to form a slick, hot little pile.

"Help me," he said, "for God's sake, Evelyn, please pick up the gun and help me."

She looked at me and then she lifted the Browning. "It's all so fucked up," she said. She raised her head and looked at me. "He's not my father. Did you know that?"

"I know."

"But I love him anyway." She was hysterical. "And now he's in such pain."

Right before it was all over, he said, "Please, let her do it, Dwyer. Please let her do it. I can't take the pain much longer."

I started for her, but she was way too fast. She did it, and there wasn't any way I could stop it and I wasn't even sure I wanted to.

When she finished she went out into the rain under the elm branches dripping cold silver, and vomited.

I went in and called the sheriff's department.

22 A WEEK LATER WE WERE WALKING DOWN A long, sunny white corridor, following a nurse who wore squeaking white shoes. We walked past a big blue statue of the Virgin to an even sunnier room where a man who resembled Stephen Wade sat on the edge of a bed holding in his right hand a cigarette smoked down to the filter and in his left a paperback book by the monk Thomas Merton.

In a week he'd lost ten pounds. He looked a little younger and a lot more scared. He put the book down and stubbed the cigarette out and then held up both hands, the fingers of his right counting five, the fingers of his left counting two. "Seven days."

"Congratulations."

"You know, I haven't gone seven days without a drink since I was a teenager." He hacked out a cigarette cough. I could see that Donna wanted to give him her standard lacerating antismoking sermon, but right then obviously wasn't the right time.

She leaned over and kissed him and then he took her in his arms and held her tight and long. Then he let her go and, weary and sad, said, "I don't know what to do."

"Go see her."

"They say the whole drying-out process takes about a month up here."

"Then go see her in a month."

He had another cigarette. "Sylvia any better?"

I shook my head.

"She may never pull out of this one," he said, referring to her total retreat into her illness. He took a big drag. The smoke was blue in the sunlight. "What's going to happen to Evelyn?"

"We're not sure. But her lawyer thinks he can make things reasonably easy for her, given the circumstances. A verdict of temporary insanity would play pretty well here."

He looked at us and frowned. "You know, I never had a clue about her being my daughter. Sylvia and I only slept with each other a couple of times, when David was away on a four-month road trip once."

Donna said, "That's how Dwyer figured it out. He kept staring at the playbill of David in that road company. Then when Dr. Kern mentioned it being Evelyn's birthday, he realized that she couldn't possibly be David's daughter because David hadn't been around."

"I never had a clue," Stephen Wade said again. He had some more of his cigarette, or it had some more of him, depending on your point of view, and then he sat back against his pillow, looking as if he were about to drop off to sleep. "I should probably spend some time with her now, huh?" he said.

"She's your daughter," I said.

"You know how goddamn funny that sounds?" he said.

"I'm fifty-three and I just learned I've got a twenty-four-year-old daughter."

"It won't be easy, Stephen," Donna said, "but I sure bet it'll be worth it."

An hour later, in the parking lot, she leaned over and kissed me and said, "Boy, Dwyer, feel the sun. Isn't it great?"

We stood there in the warm golden light, just stood for maybe two whole minutes. I sure as hell wasn't going to disagree with her.

About the Author

Edward Gorman is an advertising executive, living and working in Cedar Rapids, Iowa. He is the author of ROUGH CUT; NEW, IMPROVED MURDER; and MURDER STRAIGHT UP.